Kira and the Rat Queen

The Rainbow Princess Chronicles Book 2

by

Jason R. James

Best Wishes—

12-19-17

For my amazing nieces,

Alex, Rachel, Emily, and Eva

Table of Contents

Chapter 1: Rats

Kira opened her eyes, blinking against the sunlight. *Where was she?*

"Happy birthday, sweetheart!" Her mom sang out the words, hugging Kira tight around the shoulders and bending down to kiss her forehead. Kira could feel her mom's hair falling against her face, tickling her nose. She laughed.

Then Kira knew exactly where she was—she was standing in her own backyard. *But how did she get here?* Just a second ago she was somewhere else. She tried to remember. *Where was she just a second ago?*

Something was wrong—Kira knew that—but she didn't care. It was warm, and bright, and it was her birthday!

Kira could see the picnic table in the corner of the yard with a big chocolate cake sitting on top of it, decorated with a dozen candles. Red and blue balloons were tied to the backs of the chairs, bobbing up and down in the breeze, and Kira was surrounded by a crowd of kids from her school. They were all wearing yellow party hats—the cardboard kind shaped like cones.

"Happy birthday, honey. Are you ready for your piñata?"

Kira turned around. It was her dad. He was standing by the red maple in the backyard, holding onto a rope. It stretched over a branch of the maple, and on the other end, Kira could see her piñata dangling from the tree. It was huge—at least half as big as Kira—and it was decorated like a rainbow-colored unicorn. Her dad pulled on the rope, and the papier-mâché unicorn danced up and down in the air. Kira laughed again. So did her dad.

"Go ahead, honey," he said. "Let's bust this thing open and see what's inside."

Kira looked down at her hands. She was holding a long, wooden broom handle wrapped in purple and pink streamers—the perfect weapon to break a piñata. Kira smiled. Then she raised the stick over her head, ready to swing at the piñata, but just before she could start the stick was ripped out of her hands.

"Hey," Kira shouted as she spun around. "Why did you—"

"Why did I what?" the girl behind Kira snapped. It was Sophia Masters, and she was the one holding the broom handle now.

Sophia was the tallest, prettiest, most popular girl in Kira's class, with long, blonde hair and no freckles. In other words, she was the exact opposite of Kira.

Kira was short and plain-looking, with a sprinkle of freckles over her nose. And her hair wasn't long or blonde—it was short and pink! And Kira certainly wasn't popular… Sophia made sure of that.

Now Sophia stood tapping the broomstick against her open hand. "I don't know what you think you're doing. *I'm* a guest at this party, and that means I get to go first."

Kira looked down at her feet. "But it's my birthday."

Sophia sucked in a quick breath of air between her teeth. "That's too bad."

Then, without another word, Sophia raised the stick over her head and charged at the piñata. She hit it once, twice, a third time. WHACK! WHACK! WHACK!

The piñata split open and fell to the ground. Kira raced forward, ready to scoop up the loose candy… only there was no candy on the ground. It was just the broken piñata with a jagged gash on its side.

Then Kira heard a squeak. It was shrill, like the sound your shoe makes when you walk into school on a rainy day. It was followed by another squeak. Then another. Now the sounds were getting louder, and they all seemed to be coming from inside the piñata.

Kira dropped down onto her hands and knees, lowering her face to try and see inside the broken unicorn. She thought that maybe it was filled with toys instead of candy, maybe rubber balls that squeak, but it was too dark to see anything.

Then something crawled out of the piñata. It was tiny, only about the size of Kira's fist, and it was covered in greasy, gray fur. Its paper-thin ears were pinned back against its pointed head, and it lifted its nose to sniff the air. Kira could see its tiny pink paws and feet against the dark green grass, each finger and toe ending in a black pin for a claw, and she could see its beady, red-rimmed eyes and its long, limp tail dragging behind it.

Kira screamed and scrambled to her feet, staggering back from the piñata, but the rat followed her. It jumped forward, rising up on its back legs to sniff the air again.

Then Kira looked back at the broken unicorn lying on the ground. A second rat was wiggling its way out of the gash. It was followed by a third. Then a fourth. And now they were squeezing through the piñata two at a time, three at a time. Four at a time!

The rats ran forward. They covered the ground like a carpet. There were so many that they were running over top of each other, rolling up and down like waves in the ocean. They swarmed over Kira's feet and raced around her ankles. She could feel their fur brushing against her skin.

Then Kira heard someone scream behind her. She turned around to look. Her classmates were all running around the yard, their arms waving in the air, all of them desperate to escape from the rat stampede, but one by one, the boys and girls would trip and fall to the ground. Then the rats would wash over them, burying them in an avalanche of gray fur.

Kira looked back to Sophia. She was the last girl left, but now she had changed. Sophia didn't look like the pretty, popular girl from school anymore. Instead, her face had stretched, and it was covered in gray hair. Her eyes were round and black. She had white whiskers growing from the sides of her nose, and long, pointed teeth that curved over her lips.

Kira stepped back. “Sophia, wh-what’s happening?”

But Sophia ignored her. Instead she pointed a long, crooked finger at Kira’s dad. Then Sophia shrieked—a terrible sound, loud and shrill. It sounded to Kira like she screamed the words, “Get him!”

The rats turned their heads to look at Kira’s father. Sophia shrieked again, and they all charged. They circled around her dad’s legs, climbing up his pants, clawing their way up his shirt. There were hundreds of them all over his body.

Kira could see her dad trying to fight them off, smacking his hands left and right to keep them away, but there were too many. They were up to his shoulders now and starting to cover his head.

Kira wanted to help. She wanted to run to her father and save him, but she couldn’t move. It felt like her feet were sunk in cement. She tried to scream to her dad—she wanted to tell him to keep fighting—but she couldn’t find her voice. All she could do was stand and watch.

Then Kira's dad lost his balance and fell backwards. He landed on top of even more rats, thousands of rats, and they started running. They carried him away like he was riding on the conveyor belt at the grocery store, and there was nothing Kira could do.

"Henry!" Kira's mom screamed.

Kira turned to look in the other direction. Just like her dad, Kira's mother had fallen onto her back, and now she was being carried away by the rats. Her mom saw Kira too.

She reached out her hand and screamed again. "Help me! Kira, save me!"

But Kira still couldn't answer.

She turned back to the Rat Queen and saw the long, crooked finger pointed straight at her face.

Again, Kira tried to scream.

Chapter 2: Bacon for Breakfast

Kira sat up straight, gasping. She touched her face to make sure nothing was on it. *No rats. No scratches. She was safe.*

Kira took another deep breath. She told herself it was all a dream—the birthday, the piñata, and the rats. It was only her imagination, but knowing that didn't make Kira feel any better.

The sky above was still dark, but it was turning gray in the east—almost morning—and Kira could barely see through the shadows. She looked to her left. Lying on the ground, curled up on his side under his blankets, she could just see the top of Ben's brown hair. Kira met Ben a week ago in her dad's office, and at first, she thought he was a knight: Sir Ben the Brave. Now she knew that was all a lie. Ben was really a cook, but he still turned out to be brave, and in the end, that was more important.

Kira looked to her right. On her other side she could see Fred, asleep on his back, his eyes closed, and his mouth open and snoring. When Kira met Fred a week ago she thought he was a zombie. She was right, but Fred was also the nicest zombie you could ever hope to meet, kind and considerate and a vegetarian. Kira was glad they were with her—both of them.

She kicked off her blankets and stood up. It was still too early to be awake, but she needed to take a walk and clear her head. Kira meandered through the woods, wandering between the tall trees and climbing a small hill. At the top of the rise, she came to a clearing and without the trees in her way, she could see the whole expanse of the sky. Far in the distance it was still black night, and she could just see the twinkling stars over the horizon. Somehow it made her miss her mom and dad even more. Kira sat down on the grass.

So much had changed in just one week. Kira was a princess now, and both her parents were missing—stolen away. She had travelled through a magic portal to save them, and she beat the King of the Zombies at a spelling contest. Then she learned that her father was sold to the Queen of the Rats. Now it was up to Kira and her friends to save him. *But how?*

"Princess?"

Kira recognized the soft, growling voice behind her. She turned around and saw Snugg, her teddy bear, walking up the hill. Unlike Ben and Fred, Kira had known Snugg all of her life—although she didn't know he could move or talk until recently.

Snugg stepped closer. "Did you have another nightmare, Princess?"

Kira nodded.

"The same nightmare as before? The one with the rats?"

Kira nodded again.

Snugg sat down beside her. "Would you like a hug, Princess? Would that help?"

Then Snugg stretched out his arms and Kira scooped him up, squeezing the tiny bear tight, and Snugg hugged his soft, furry arms around Kira's neck.

Kira could feel warm tears start to fill her eyes. "I want my dad, Snugg. I want to save him."

"I know that, Princess," Snugg answered, hugging Kira tighter. "And we'll find a way. I promise you, we'll find a way to save your dad together."

Kira pulled away, wiping her hand across her eyes. She wanted to believe Snugg—she knew the bear meant what he said—but right now it all sounded impossible. *How would they ever save her dad from the Rat Queen?*

"Are you ready to go back to camp, Princess?" Snugg asked.

Kira climbed slowly back to her feet. The sky above them wasn't dark anymore—not even in the west. Everything had been washed with the dull gray of morning. That meant it was time to start their day—whether Kira was ready or not. She nodded her head at the bear.

"Then follow me," Snugg said, and he turned for camp.

As Kira and Snugg wound their way between the trees, a familiar smell drifted up into her nose. It was warm and sizzling—the smell of bacon. She could hear it too, the crackling grease popping inside the pan. It reminded Kira of her dad. He would always wake up early on Sunday mornings to cook breakfast. Kira would stumble down the stairs, still half-asleep and wearing her pajamas, and she would find her dad standing over the stove—scrambled eggs and bacon cooking on the left and pancakes on the griddle on the right.

Kira would drop into her seat at the kitchen table, and her glass of orange juice would already be waiting for her. she would say, "Morning, Chef."

Then her dad would turn around and smile. "Morning, Sweets."

Kira was still thinking about the pancakes and orange juice when another smell reached her nose, and then her whole face wrinkled up—it was lima beans, corn, and carrots. Thankfully her dad never made *that* in the morning.

Kira and Snugg turned past another tree trunk, and then she could see the camp. Ben was kneeling over a low fire, cooking the breakfast, and Fred was standing just past him, rolling up their blankets.

As Kira and Snugg stepped forward, Ben rose to his feet, still holding the pan with the bacon. "You're back. Just in time."

Fred stopped in the middle of rolling a blanket. "Did you have the nightmare again, Your Highness?"

Kira nodded.

"Breakfast will help with that. Come on," Ben said, nodding toward the cooking fire.

Kira, Snugg, and Fred all found their seats. Then Ben used a fork to place two strips of bacon on three of the plates. The fourth plate he filled with the vegetable mash. Finally, he took out four biscuits from his bag and handed one to each of his friends, saving the last for himself.

"Eat up." Ben took a big bite of his biscuit. "This is the last of our food. All we have left are lima beans. We still have plenty of those."

Fred raised his spoon, and it was filled with vegetables. "That sounds good to me."

Ben looked at the zombie. "You think we'll reach a village today? Or a farm? I'd rather not starve out here in the wilderness."

Fred laughed. "We're not going to starve. We should reach the village of Stony Pointe before lunch. We can find food there."

Then the zombie looked across the fire at Kira. "Was it the same dream, Your Highness?"

Kira sat still, holding her piece of bacon to her lips without taking a bite. "It was exactly the same. It started with Sophia at my birthday party. Then she changed into the Rat Queen and her rats attacked us—thousands of them. And I could feel them this time—all of them—crawling over me."

Kira shivered at the memory and threw her bacon down on her plate.

Snugg cleared his throat. "You know, Your Highness, we're not sure the Rat Queen can even control her rats. They may just live with her, like pets."

"But you don't *know* that!" Kira wheeled around to face Snugg, and her voice was louder and sharper than she intended. "There was no Rat Queen when you and Fred were here, and Ben told us he never met her before. So we don't *know* anything!"

"We know she's crazy," Ben said, stuffing the last bite of his biscuit into his mouth. Then the other three all looked at him, and Ben realized his mistake. He forced himself to swallow, and then he tried to recover. "I don't mean she's scary-crazy. We don't know what kind of crazy she is. I mean, I guess she could be scary-crazy, but that's not what I'm saying. I'm just… Everyone says she's crazy, and I'm saying that we don't know what kind—"

Kira slammed her plate down on the ground. "Great! So, we know she's crazy, but we don't know how to rescue my father! We've been walking for three days and we still don't have a plan to save him."

Everyone looked down at their plates, because there was nothing more to say. Kira was right. They had been working on a rescue plan for three straight days, but it was impossible to plan a rescue when they knew so little.

Finally, Fred rose to his feet. "Your Highness, we should practice with your sword before we start walking for the day. Don't you think?"

Kira nodded. "All right. Let me clear my plate."

"I'll take care of it for you." Ben reached for Kira's plate. "And I'll take care of that biscuit, too—you haven't even touched it."

Kira handed her biscuit to the boy. "You should forget about the dishes and come with us. You haven't practiced swords for the last two days."

Ben shook his head. "I'm no good with a sword. You saw me the first day, tripping over my own feet. You were a thousand times better than me."

Kira's face twisted. "But that's why we practice. We train ourselves to get better."

Ben laughed. "I don't have it in me. It was the same thing with the Knights. All the other boys could make shields of light and swords of light. Meanwhile, I could barely gather enough light to make a ball."

"Wait a minute," Kira said, looking down at Ben. "You said—you said you couldn't build anything from the light."

"Nobody cares about a ball of light." Ben turned away, scraping the food on Kira's plate into the fire. "It was embarrassing to keep failing, so I stopped trying—same way I've stopped trying with those swords. Just let me be the cook, all right? I'm good at that."

Kira was ready to answer, but then a hand on her shoulder made her stop. She turned around and saw Fred standing behind her, shaking his head.

The zombie forced a smile. "We'll ask him again tomorrow—that's the best we can do. As for today, *you're* the one who needs to train."

Kira nodded. "Then I'm ready."

Chapter 3: Sword Lessons

Kira wrapped her belt around her waist and drew her sword. Then she turned the weapon quickly through the air, left and right, admiring the blade.

The sword itself was long, thin, and pointy—just like Fred's sword—with a silver swept hilt and a wire-wrapped handle. Fred told her this type of sword was called a rapier, and he said that if she was going to carry it, she might as well know how to use it. That's why they had been practicing every morning for the last three days.

Kira followed Fred away from the camp until finally the zombie stopped in a small clearing of flat land. Then he drew his sword and turned to face her.

Fred smiled. “I wonder what your father would say about all of this, Your Highness—about you learning to fight with a sword?”

Kira laughed to herself, because she knew *exactly* what her father would say. They never talked about swords, specifically, but they had talked about fighting only a year ago.

Kira remembered she was in fourth grade, and her dad was picking her up early to go to the dentist. When they got to his car to leave the school, Kira was almost in tears.

Her dad turned around in his seat and looked at her. “What’s wrong, Sweets?”

Kira shook her head. She didn’t want to say it out loud, but she couldn’t hold it in, either. Then everything spilled out like water breaking through a dam, her words tumbling out in a jumbled mess. “Sophia made up a song about me. They were singing it all day. Calling me a baby because I have a teddy bear, and making fun of my hair. They wouldn't stop. I wanted to push her down and make her stop—"

"Did you?"

"Did I what?"

Her dad reached behind his seat and held Kira's hand. "Did you really push her down?"

Kira shook her head. "No… I just wanted to."

Her dad leaned over his seat and kissed Kira on her forehead. "Then I'm proud of you, Sweets. Pushing someone—or kicking them or punching them—doesn't solve our problems. You need to be smarter, braver, kinder, and that's much harder to do than pushing."

Kira lowered her eyes. Now she felt bad for even *wanting* to push Sophia, but her dad wasn't finished.

He squeezed her hand, and suddenly, his voice was hard. "But listen to me, Kira. If anyone ever tries to hurt you—you or any of your friends—you fight them. You fight and you win. No one's ever allowed to hurt you."

Kira shook her head. "How will I know? How will I know when to fight and when to talk?"

Her dad turned back around in his seat and started the car. "You're a smart girl, Kira. I trust you to know the difference."

"And how will I win."

Her dad laughed in the front seat. "You win by trying—that's all any of us can do. But… I have a couple moves I can show you, if you want."

Then Kira's memory faded, and she was back in the present, standing across from Fred.

She raised her sword in front of her face in salute. "My dad would say that violence doesn't solve our problems, but if I need to defend myself with a sword, I'd better win."

Fred raised his own sword in salute. "Then your father's a smart man. Now, Your Highness, do you remember our lessons from yesterday?"

Kira slashed her blade down toward the ground, and it made a short whistling sound as it cut the air. "I remember."

Fred repeated the lesson anyway. "Sword fighting starts on the ground. It begins with the legs—your feet. Footwork. Timing. Balance. Speed. Power. It all starts with the legs."

Kira stepped back with her left foot and raised her sword, pointing the tip at Fred's nose. "I told you, I remember."

Fred smiled. "Then show me."

The zombie swung his sword down for Kira's head, but she shuffled back, raised her blade, and blocked it. Fred swung again. This time Kira blocked to the left. Another swing. Kira turned and blocked to the right. Then Fred swung again, and again, and again. Kira blocked them all.

Fred shouted, still swinging his sword. "Why are you waiting?"

Kira shouted back, "You told me to be patient!"

Fred stabbed forward with his sword, but Kira jumped to the side and parried with her blade. "Waiting is lazy. Patience is knowing when to *stop* waiting—when to attack. Like now!"

Kira lunged forward, slashing her sword up at the zombie's head, but Fred parried and grabbed Kira by the wrist.

Then he smiled. "That was better—much better. You're learning."

Kira relaxed her arms and legs—the sparring was over, at least for now. "Should we try it again? I can do even better."

Fred shook his head. "We should get back to the others. There's still a long walk ahead of us before we reach Stony Pointe, and if we don't get there by lunch… Well, you know how Ben gets when he's hungry."

Kira laughed and nodded her head. As much as she wanted to keep practicing, nothing was more important than reaching her dad. She returned her sword to her belt and followed Fred back to camp.

Snugg looked up at them as they reached the fire. "How did the princess do today?"

Fred picked up one of the canteens from the ground, took a quick drink, and wiped his mouth with the back of his hand. "I can tell you that Ben's right about one thing: when it comes to the sword, the princess is a natural."

"Of course she is," Snugg growled.

Then a loud scream broke through the forest. "Y'all stay back or else!"

Kira was confused. *Was someone shouting at her?* Then she realized the voice was too far away. Someone was shouting, and they sounded angry, but it had nothing to do with Kira or her friends. She turned to look at Snugg. "What was that?"

"That was trouble. Everyone follow me." Snugg climbed to his feet. Then the tiny bear started in a dead sprint, dodging past trees and jumping over tangled roots. Fred followed after him, running as fast as he could into the forest, but even the long-legged zombie had a hard time keeping up with the tiny bear.

Kira started to run too, but after a couple steps, Ben shouted after her, "Wait for me!"

He was kicking dirt onto the fire. Then he gave a nod, and together, Kira and Ben started running in the same direction as Fred and Snugg. They were well behind now, and it was difficult to see the zombie and the bear as they darted between the distant trees. Then, in the next second, they were both gone—completely out of sight. Kira and Ben kept running, forcing themselves to go even faster.

Kira and Ben broke through the tree line. Now they were running through an open field under the clear blue sky and the blinding light of morning. She could see Snugg and Fred just in front of her, standing still, staring across the field.

Kira stopped next to Snugg and bent over at the waist, her hands on her knees, panting to catch her breath. She had never run that fast in her whole life. Her hair felt wet and heavy with sweat, and she was desperate for a drink of water, but there was no time for that now.

Another scream broke through the air—the same voice. "I'm warning you!"

Kira looked at Snugg. "What is it? What's wrong?"

The tiny bear pointed across the field. "It's over there, and it's just like I said… trouble."

Chapter 4: Trouble at the Farm

Kira looked in the direction Snugg was pointing, and she could see the trouble for herself. Across the field, she could see a small farmhouse painted white with red shutters, and standing in front of the house, she could see a girl.

The girl looked young, but she was much taller than Kira. Her long, dark hair was pulled back in two braided pigtails, and she wore blue jeans and a red plaid shirt. She was still too far away to see her face, but Kira thought the girl looked angry—probably because of the large frying pan the girl held over her shoulder, ready to swing like a baseball bat.

Kira could also see the target of the girl's anger. Three grown men stood in front of her. The shortest man, on the right, had spiky black hair, and the man on the left had long blonde hair pulled back in a ponytail. The man in the middle, the tallest of the three, was completely bald, and the sun reflected off his smooth scalp.

Snugg raised his paw to his mouth, signaling the others to keep quiet. Then he started forward. Kira, Ben, and Fred all followed, slowly walking through the field.

Then Kira could hear voices; it was the young girl, and she was screaming again. "I already told you, my grandpa's not here!"

The bald man shouted back, and his voice sounded rough, like sandpaper. "And we told you that doesn't matter. You need to pay us our money!"

"We ain't gotchyer money!" the girl shot back. "That's why my grandpa went to the market. He'll be coming back with your money in a week."

"You get back in that house, girl, and find our money, or we'll go in there and find it for ourselves." The bald man pointed his thick finger at the house.

But the girl raised her frying pan over her shoulder. "You take one more step toward that house and you'll kiss the backside of this skillet!"

Ben stopped walking and grabbed Snugg by the arm. He pointed at the bald man. "I know that guy. He was with Pike and the steam bandits when you were captured. He was one of them."

Snugg looked at the boy. "Are you sure?"

Ben nodded.

Then a thin smile started across Snugg's face. "Kira, Ben—I want you both to stay back. Fred and I will go and say hello."

Then the zombie and the bear started again through the field.

Kira could hear the bald man shouting, "I'm not going to ask you again, girl. You go inside and get our money!"

But before the girl could answer, Snugg roared, "That's enough!"

The three men turned on their heels, and the bald man shouted back, "Who said that?"

But Snugg kept walking forward, moving quicker now, closing the distance between them. He growled, "You don't remember me?"

Then Kira could see the bald man's eyes—of course he remembered. He reached down for his sword, but before he could pull the blade from its sheath, Snugg started running.

He popped his claws out of his tiny stuffed paws and roared. "You remember me now?"

Then Snugg leapt forward, launching himself through the air at the man's face. The bald man yelped, and then his voice was lost, muffled against Snugg's brown fur as the bear grabbed the bald man by both of his ears. The bald man stumbled back, falling to the ground with Snugg still latched around his face. Then Kira couldn't see them anymore.

The other two men looked at Fred and drew their swords. Kira had never seen anything like their weapons before in her life. The blades looked heavy and rusted, with a deep serrated edge on one side, like someone glued a handsaw to the end of a metal stick. Then she heard the noise—a high-pitched whine like a dentist's drill, and the swords started shaking, the serrated edge sliding back and forth like an electric carving knife.

Fred stood with his hands raised above his head. "You don't have to do this. You can put those swords down. You can still surrender."

But the spiky-haired man screamed and charged forward. Fred drew his rapier and parried, letting the man run past him like a bull running through a matador's red cape.

Then the blonde man swung his sword at Fred. The zombie raised his blade and blocked it. He parried another sword thrust and turned to the side. Then he swung his rapier at the blonde man's head, the thin blade darting left and right. It reminded Kira of a swarm of bees, their stingers coming from every direction, and the sound of ringing metal—sword against sword—filled the air.

It was too much for the spiky-haired man. Rather than rejoin the fight, he turned and started to run.

"Kira, get behind me," Ben screamed.

The spiky-haired steam bandit was running right for them, his sword raised above his head. Ben ran forward to meet him, drawing his own sword. He swung at the spiky-haired man, but the steam bandit was ready for him. He turned Ben's sword aside. Then he stuck out his leg, catching Ben by the ankle and tripping the boy to the ground. The spiky-haired man raised his sword again.

"You leave him alone!" Kira shouted as she drew her rapier.

The spiky-haired man turned around, his sword still poised above his head. Now, for the first time, Kira could get a good look at the man. Even though he looked shorter than the others, he was still taller than Kira. His nose tapered out to a thin point, his eyes were small, and his right ear stood out from the side of his head.

He looked at Kira and smiled. "Whatever you say, girly. I'd rather fight you anyway."

Kira felt her heart racing inside her chest, and for a second, she thought she might throw up. She had never been in a real fight, let alone a fight with swords. *What if she made a mistake?*

Suddenly, the steam bandit swung his sword at her face. Kira jumped back, and the blade cut harmlessly through the air. The man swung again, and Kira was surprised at how slow he seemed to be moving. He swung again, this time aiming at her side. Kira lifted her own sword and blocked.

Then, all at once, she understood. The spiky-haired man was bigger and stronger, but he was sloppy with the sword. Kira was quick, patient, and precise.

The man lurched forward and swung his sword again, but this time he crossed his legs, and Kira saw her chance. She lunged at the man, stabbing the point of her sword at his belly. The spiky-haired man twisted away, trying to avoid Kira's sword, but then his feet tangled under him and he fell to the ground.

Kira stood over him, the sharp point of her rapier pointed down at his chest. "Drop your sword and surrender."

Then Ben was back on his feet, standing shoulder to shoulder with Kira, his own sword pointed down at the man. "You heard the princess. Surrender."

The spiky-haired man scrambled back to his feet, shaking his head. "I'm Jagan Stone of the Westwood Steam Bandits, and I'm not surrendering to either one of you. In fact, I'm gonna cut you both open like a pair of pork chops—"

CLANG!

Jagan's eyes went blank, as if he were staring a thousand yards away. His sword dropped from his hand, and he fell to his knees. For a second, the man seemed to sway back and forth, like a bowling pin deciding if it should tip over, but then he pitched forward, landing unconscious, face down in the dirt.

The dark-haired girl with the frying pan stood behind him. "That's what you get! Now you other two, drop your swords or I'll give you more of the same!"

The corner of Kira's mouth lifted into a half-smile. "We just saved you. We're not your enemies."

"I don't know that." The girl raised her frying pan back over her shoulder. "For all I know, you may be part of his same gang!"

Ben shook his head. "That doesn't make sense. Why would we be fighting a member of our own gang?"

The girl lowered her frying pan, and her eyebrows knit together. "Well… maybe you're some kind of rival gang. It don't matter. You drop those swords, or else."

The girl lifted the pan above her head again, slowly turning it in small circles. "I'm gonna count to three…"

Kira didn't want to attack the girl with her sword, but she didn't want to get smacked in the face with a frying pan either. She needed help.

Kira looked across the field and saw Fred. Twenty yards away, the zombie was still dueling with the blonde steam bandit.

She shouted, "Fred, we need your help!"

Without missing a beat, the zombie changed his fighting tactic. Before, he was holding his ground, blocking the attacks by the steam bandit, but now he was the one pressing the advantage, moving forward, and the blonde-haired thug was stumbling back on his heels.

Their swords crossed, and Fred turned his wrist in a quick circle. Then, with a final flourish of his blade, he sent the steam bandit's sword flying out of his hand. The man raised both his arms in surrender.

Fred touched his rapier to the man's chest. "I would run away now if I were you."

The blonde thug listened. Without saying a word, he turned and started in a dead sprint across the field, running toward the forest as fast as his feet could carry him.

Fred turned to Kira and Ben, but the girl with the frying pan must have seen him out of the corner of her eye.

She wheeled around. "You stay back! I'm not afraid of no zombies, neither."

Fred stopped dead in his tracks.

"So now what?" Ben called to the zombie.

Fred shrugged. "Well, I'm not sure exactly sure. I think we could try… but then ,I don't want this girl to get hurt. I mean, I guess we could try." Then Fred gave up, and instead he shouted, "Snugg, we need your help!"

Kira looked across the field in the direction of Snugg. She could hear noises—a low growl and a few muffled screams—but she couldn't see the tiny bear. Suddenly, Snugg's head popped up over the tall grass. A second later, the bald man stood up behind him, staggering to his feet. The man's face looked bruised, swollen, and bloody, and Kira thought he looked like he was crying. She could see streaks of dirt under both of his eyes. Snugg must have been attacking the man with his fists and claws the entire time they were fighting.

For a moment, the bald man stared at Snugg, and Kira could tell he was angry. He was probably thinking about tackling the bear from behind, but then he must have thought better of it. Instead of running at Snugg, the bald man turned away and ran toward the forest.

Snugg growled over his shoulder, “Good riddance.” Then he looked back at his friends. “What’s the problem?”

The girl with the frying pan stepped back, turning to face Snugg. “I don’t know who you think you are, but you can just stay back too.”

Snugg stared at the girl. “And I don’t know who you are, but I came here to face the Rat Queen. Either you drop that frying pan and stand out of our way, or you start using it.”

Then the girl’s entire attitude changed. Her eyebrows lifted, and she dropped her skillet to the ground. “You’re here to stop the Rat Queen? Why didn’t you say so?”

Chapter 5: Chloe

Snugg stared at the girl. "Well then, if we're not going to be enemies, maybe you can tell us who you are and why you picked a fight with three steam bandits."

"That's easy enough." The girl smiled. "Those men thought they'd get inside my grandpa's house, and I wasn't letting nobody in without an invitation. We were just about to sort things out when y'all showed up. Guess I'm grateful you did. As for who I am, that's simple too. Name's Chloe."

"It's nice to meet you, Chloe," the teddy bear growled, reaching out to shake the girl's hand. "My name's Snugg, and I serve as the royal guard to—"

Before the bear could start reciting all of her names and titles, Kira jumped forward, shaking Chloe's hand. "I'm Kira, and you can call me Kira, but I'm also a Rainbow Princess."

Chloe laughed. "Sure you are! And I guess that makes me Queen of the Fairies!"

Kira stepped back. "No, really. I'm a princess."

"Of course she's a princess," Snugg growled. "You happen to be speaking to Princess Kira the First, Defender of the Kingdoms, Lady of the Unicorn Spire—"

Then Chloe's face drained of color. "You mean… You're saying—you're really who you say you are?"

"I'm afraid so," Kira smiled.

"Well, I just—" Chloe stuck out her arm to shake hands again, but then she thought better of it and pulled her arm back, trying to sink into a deep curtsey instead. "I mean— Your Majesty."

Kira felt her face get warm. It was strange having a girl her own age call her "Your Majesty." Kira shook her head. "I would much rather you keep calling me Kira. That's my name, after all."

Chloe rose back up to her full height. "Okay then, Kira. If that's what you want." Then she turned to look at Ben and Fred. "And what's their story?"

Fred bowed deeply at the waist. "Well, my name's Fred—Fred the zombie. I was in exile for a long time, but now I'm back and regent of the Zombie Kingdom. Funny how that works, I guess."

Chloe laughed. "Well, you sound like the fanciest zombie I ever met, that's for sure." Then she looked over at Ben. "And what does that make you? You must be a prince or a knight or something?"

"I'm none of those things," Ben said. "My name's Ben, and I'm only the cook."

Chloe curtsied again. "Well, it's nice to meet you anyway, Ben the Cook."

Ben bowed at the waist. "And it's nice to meet you, Chloe with the Frying Pan."

"Yep. I guess that's as good a name as any for me." Chloe reached down and picked her skillet up from the grass. She twirled it over in her hand. "Works just as good as your sword, I suppose."

Ben's face turned dark red, but Chloe failed to notice.

She turned instead to Kira. "Now maybe you can tell me what your business is with the Rat Queen."

Kira felt her stomach twist inside her, like even saying the words out loud might make her sick, but she had to answer. "The Rat Queen has my father. She's holding him prisoner, and we're on our way to get him back."

Then Chloe's smile fell away. "Is that— is that really the truth?"

Snugg nodded. "And the problem is, we don't know anything about this Rat Queen… only rumors. Anything you could tell us—anything at all—might prove invaluable."

Before Chloe could answer, the steam bandit lying on the ground made a low, growling noise, his face still pressed flat against the ground. It reminded

Kira of the sound she made every morning waking up for school: a painful groan of resignation.

Chloe looked back at Snugg. “I’ll tell you what. Stony Pointe is just five miles west of here. If you all help me take this man into the sheriff, I’ll tell you everything I know about the Rat Queen on our way. What d’you say? We got a deal?”

“Deal,” Kira answered, stretching out her arm to shake hands with Chloe.

“All right then,” Chloe said, smiling. Then she took Kira’s hand. “Y’all gather your things, and I’ll lock up the house and we can get started.”

It took more effort than they thought to get the spiky-haired man back on his feet, and even once he stood up, he staggered back as if he were dizzy. Fred had to grab him under one of his arms, and Ben took the other, steadying the man between them.

Then, finally, they started off with Snugg leading the way across the field. Kira and Chloe walked a few paces behind him, side by side as if they had been friends for a long time. Ben, Fred, and the prisoner, Jagan, brought up the rear.

At first no one spoke, but as they stepped onto the shaded trail winding its way through the forest, Chloe cleared her throat. "Our kingdom is called the Garden. It's the smallest in the Rainbow Kingdoms, but we don't mind. We have great farmland and a bit of the coast, and people have always been able to earn a living. That's what mattered, but that was before the Rat Queen.

"It used to be that Princess Indigo was in charge of the Garden, but you probably already knew that. I mean, she's *your* aunt after all."

Kira shook her head. "No, not really."

A week ago, Kira didn't think she had any aunts—or uncles, cousins, or grandparents for that matter. It was always just her and her parents, but that was before she stepped through the magical portal. That's when she learned about Princess Saphron, the woman in charge of the Rainbow Kingdoms, and now, apparently, there was a second aunt—some woman named Indigo. *How many more secret relatives could she have?*

Chloe shrugged. "Well, after the Rainbow King disappeared and Saphron took over, Princess Indigo—she just left us. That's when the Rat Queen took charge."

"And what did she do?" Kira asked.

Chloe shook her head. "Listen, I never met the woman—never even seen her—but I can tell you for a fact, the Rat Queen is crazy!"

"Wait a minute," Ben called out from behind. "What do you mean, you've never even seen her?"

Chloe looked over her shoulder. "No one has. She's locked herself away in the Rat Fort, and the only person she allows inside is Mayor Randolph, the leader of Stony Pointe.

Kira was confused. "But if you've never seen her for yourself, how do you know she's crazy?"

"Because of how she's running the Garden!" Chloe said. "The first thing she did, she started paying us buckets of gold for any extra milk—which was the good kind of crazy, but still crazy. Then she raised our taxes. She started collecting from us twice a week, and she hired these steam bandits to make sure we pay."

"And that's why those men were at your grandpa's house?" Kira asked.

Chloe nodded. "When we can't pay with money, they break into our homes and take whatever they want—food, clothes, furniture. It doesn't matter, as long as we pay."

Snugg stopped and turned around. "If the steam bandits work for the Rat Queen, what will she say about this one going to jail?"

Jagan started laughing from the back of the column—a loud, rolling sound like someone had just told him the funniest joke in the world.

"What's so funny?" Snugg roared.

The steam bandit caught his breath. "It's just—I mean it's you—all of you. You're so worried about this Rat Queen."

"And what should we be worried about? You?" Kira crossed her arms and stared back at him.

Jagan shook his head and chuckled. "No. not me, girlie. Didn't you hear what I said before? I'm part of the Westwood Steam Bandits. You know what Pike's gonna do when he finds out that you captured one of his men? He's gonna burn that poor girl's farm to the ground. He may burn down all of Stony Pointe village. Maybe he'll let me light the match."

Kira closed her eyes. Just hearing the man's name—Pike—was enough to send a shiver down her back. Kira hated the man. She was afraid of him, and she hated the fact that she was afraid of him.

She imagined Pike with his eyes covered by those round, thick goggles, his greasy, black hair falling back over his head, and his pale, crooked teeth filling the bottom half of his face. Then Kira shivered again, and this time, Jagan saw her.

"That's right, girlie," he said, smiling. "You *should* be scared of Pike. When he gets done with you, I promise it won't be pretty."

"That's enough out of you," Snugg growled.

Then Jagan looked at the bear, still smiling. "I'll keep quiet for now, but don't say I didn't warn you."

Chloe shook her head. "It doesn't matter—not even if they burn our farm. Grandpa says if things don't change soon, we'll have to leave the Garden for good."

"Isn't there anything you can do?" Fred asked as they started again through the forest. "Have you sent word to Princess Saphron? Maybe she can help."

Chloe laughed. "We already sent her a letter asking for help, but she said she won't get involved. She says it's not her problem." Chloe looked down at the dirt and shook her head. "No… I'm afraid we're on our own."

The trail through the forest sloped gently upward, and as the companions reached the crest of the hill, they stepped once more out of the woods. Now they stood at the edge of another field, a blanket of green grass and yellow wildflowers laid out before them, and at the bottom of the hill, Kira could see a village.

Dirt roads crisscrossed between a handful of simple wooden buildings, and from the closest building, Kira could see smoke curling into the sky from the chimney. She took a deep breath. The air smelled like warm bread—bread and salt water!

Kira looked to her left. She had no idea they were so close to the ocean, but now, from the top of the hill, she could see blue-gray water rippling in the bay, sparkling in the sunlight. But that wasn't all. She could also see a low, stone bridge stretching over the water, and in the middle of the bay, rising from the water, the towering black walls of a castle.

Kira felt someone's hand touch her shoulder. She turned around, and Chloe was standing next to her. "First we take this steam bandit to the sheriff. Then we go to the Rat Fort and get your dad. Do we have a deal?"

Kira nodded. "Deal."

Chapter 6: Old Enemies

Kira followed Chloe into the village. Ben, Fred, Snugg, and Jagan all trailed behind. Chloe led them down a dirt road. Then she turned to her left and opened the door of a low, wooden building. Kira stepped inside.

In the center of the room, immediately in front of Kira, she could see a man seated behind a desk. He looked tall and thin with a bushy mustache of orange and gray hair overgrowing his top lip. He wore a brown, buttoned shirt with a copper star pinned to his chest, and a brown cowboy hat on top of his head.

The man pushed up the brim of his hat with his finger. "Can I help you, miss?"

Before Kira could answer, Jagan stumbled into the room behind her, followed by Ben, Fred, and Snugg.

The man behind the desk jumped to his feet. "What in tarnation's going on here?"

"Arrest that man, Sheriff Quincy." Chloe stepped into the room and slammed the door behind her.

Then the sheriff rolled his eyes, shook his head, and sat back down in his chair. "Dagnabbit, Chloe! You know I can't go arrestin' this man."

Chloe pushed her way past the others to stand in front of the desk. "And why not, Quincy? Your jail full again?"

Kira looked past the Sheriff toward the back of the room. She could see gray metal bars running from the ceiling to the floor, dividing the room in half. Behind the bars, there was an old cot with a pillow on top of it, and a wooden chair with only three legs. And that was it. Other than the furniture, the cell was empty, and judging by the thick layer of dust coating the floor behind the bars, it had been empty for a long time.

Sheriff Quincy shook his head. “Now Chloe, I tol’ your Grandpa I’d look out for you. What would he say if he saw you here?”

“He’d say, ‘Arrest that man, Sheriff.’” Chloe stamped her foot on the floor.

“I can’t arrest him and you know it.” Sheriff Quincy pushed back from his desk and climbed again to his feet. “He ain’t done nothing wrong ‘cept get caught by you, and that ain’t exactly a crime.”

“He attacked me,” Chloe shouted.

Jagan shook his head. “Actually, she’s the one who attacked me.”

Sheriff Quincy ignored him. Instead, the sheriff stepped around his desk, hunched over at the shoulders, and leaned in to look closer at Chloe, closing one of his eyes. It reminded Kira of someone trying to read tiny handwriting from far away.

After a second, the sheriff stepped back and stood up. “Now you tell me the truth. Did that man attack you, or was he just talkin' loud so you got yer fryin' pan?"

Chloe stamped her foot, and now her face was turning bright red. "He attacked me. And then he said he was gonna burn down our farm. That's a threat! Just ask Kira about that part."

Sheriff Quincy shook his head again. "And who's Kira supposed to be? Who are any of these people for that matter? We don't get many teddy bears or zombies in Stony Pointe, and I think you're probably the first girl with pink hair I've ever seen in my life—"

Kira could feel her face get hot. She hated talking about her pink hair. In fact, she would rather talk about almost anything else.

Now she stepped forward and stuck out her arm to shake hands. "It's nice to meet you. I'm Kira, and I'm one of Chloe's friends—"

"No. That's not your name," a deep voice purred behind her. "You're *Princess* Kira, Defender of the Kingdoms, Lady of the blah, blah, blech."

Kira recognized the voice. She spun around on her heels, and Ben, Fred, and Snugg all did the same. Then she saw him standing just inside the door of the sheriff's office. It was Pike. He wore his long brown coat, the bottom of it caked with mud. His greasy black hair fell around his face with his rumpled top hat perched to one side of his head. He looked exactly the same as he did in Kira's imagination, only he wasn't smiling and the thick goggles he wore over his eyes were lifted up, resting on his forehead. Then, for the first time, Kira could see his eyes. They were black, small, and round, like onyx pearls set back in his head.

Two men stood beside Pike, one on either side. On his right, it was the tall, bald man from Chloe's farm. His face was still bruised and cut from his battle with Snugg. Now he stared down at the floor in front of him, and Kira thought he looked like a dog that's been yelled at for stealing food.

On the other side of Pike stood a man that Kira had never seen before. He was older than the others, with feathery gray hair on top of his head. He was a big man too, barrel-chested and potbellied. He wore a short gray beard over the bottom half of his face, and his eyes were blue. From the moment Kira turned around, he had been staring at her.

Pike stepped forward, doffing his hat with a flourish and bowing deeply at the waist. Now, at last, he was smiling—the same smile filled with pale, crooked teeth. "It's good to see you again, Kira."

Kira felt her stomach twist and tighten as soon as Pike said her name. She remembered the first time she met the steam bandit. He knew Kira's name then, too, but how was that possible? Kira *never* told Pike her name. *How could he know so much about her?*

Snugg jumped in front of Kira, his claws out and ready. "Get behind me, Princess."

Pike looked down at the teddy bear, but he spoke to the bald man standing next to him. "Is he the one who messed up your face?"

The bald man nodded. "That's him. He's got those claws—"

"Oh, I can see," Pike purred, still smiling. "This little guy is absolutely *terrifying*."

Kira could see Pike wasn't afraid of Snugg. In fact, when he said the word "terrifying," she was sure he meant the opposite. Kira could hear Snugg start to growl.

Then Ben shouted, "Get out of here, Pike! You have no business here."

Now Pike laughed, and he nodded his head toward Ben. "Look over there, Brog. It's the cook. I was hoping to meet you again, Mr. Cook." Then Pike's voice fell to a hiss. "We still owe you for our *dinner.*"

Now there was no mistaking the threat behind the steam bandit's words. It made Kira feel sick to her stomach again.

Pike pointed at Jagan, standing to the side of the room. "As for my business, Mr. Cook, that man over there *is* my business."

"What's going on Mayor Randolph?" Sheriff Quincy pushed up the brim of his hat.

Now it was the old man's turn to speak. Randolph stepped forward and pulled his hand across his gray beard. "Mr. Pike got word that three of his men were attacked. He heard that this one," Randolph pointed at Jagan in the corner, "got captured. Pike wants his man released."

"You can't do that!" Kira cried out before she could stop herself. Suddenly, everyone in the room was looking at her.

For a second, she hesitated—maybe it wasn't her place to contradict the mayor and the sheriff. Then again, Kira was also a Rainbow Princess, and letting Jagan go wasn't right. She needed to say something.

Kira took a deep breath. "Everything Chloe told you is the truth. This man threatened to burn down her farm. He said he would burn the entire village. You can't just let him go."

Pike smiled even wider. "You want to explain to Kira how things work here in the Garden, Mayor Randolph, or should I do it?"

Randolph cleared his throat. "Mr. Pike and his Westwood Steam Bandits are the chosen agents of the Rat Queen. Therefore, they are granted immunity from all our laws. This man is free to go."

Jagan laughed. Then he walked across the room to stand next to the bald man. "You understand what all that means, Princess? It means I could burn this village down tonight, and there's not a thing you could do to stop me."

"I wouldn't be so sure of that." Ben stepped up next to Kira.

Jagan laughed again. "You already tried once, cook. You fell face down in the dirt. Remember that?"

Ben's face went bright red at the memory, but he was still smiling. "I know what happened. I know you got knocked out cold by a frying pan. You remember that?"

Then Jagan's face clouded over—his smile was gone, and his eyebrows folded down over his eyes.

"That's enough," Pike hissed. "Jagan, Brog, go wait outside. You've both done enough."

The bald man and Jagan turned without either one speaking a word. Then they walked out of the sheriff's office.

Pike waited for the door to close behind them. "Now, Mayor Randolph, explain the rest."

Kira was confused. *Pike already got what he wanted. What more could there be?*

But Mayor Randolph understood. The old man nodded. "You should know it's against the law to interfere with Mr. Pike or any of his men as they perform their duties for the Rat Queen. If either one of these girls or their friends attack the steam bandits again, they're to be arrested."

"Sheriff Quincy wouldn't do that!" Chloe shouted.

"Sheriff Quincy will follow the law," Randolph barked back at the girl.

Kira's skin felt cold, and she balled up both of her fists to stop herself from shivering. She didn't want Pike to know she was angry, or scared, or anything.

But the steam bandit only smiled, baring his crooked teeth. "And I think that concludes our business, Mr. Mayor. I'll be back at the end of the week for your taxes."

Pike bowed again at the waist. Then he turned and left the room.

Kira unclenched her fists and looked down. Her hands were still shaking.

Chapter 7: Mayor Randolph

Mayor Randolph took a deep breath. Then he turned to look at Kira. “Princess, are you all right?”

Kira’s face twisted. “What?”

Randolph’s concern didn’t make any sense. Just a second ago, he was standing shoulder to shoulder with Pike, threatening to have Kira and all her friends arrested. Now he was asking if she was okay.

Kira looked over at Snugg and Fred. The tiny bear lifted both his eyebrows, and the zombie shrugged his shoulders. They looked even more lost than Kira.

But not Ben—Ben was angry. He shouted back at the mayor. "What do you care if she's all right?"

"Oh, no—" Mayor Randolph shook his head, raising both of his hands out in front of him. "No, no, no… Please, friends, try to understand the position I'm in."

"Then explain it to us." Fred said, taking a step closer to Kira.

"Of course." Randolph pulled his hand through his gray beard. "It's just, I'm the only person allowed to speak with the Rat Queen—the only outsider she trusts. But my first loyalty lies to the people of the Garden… and the Rainbow Family, of course."

"You didn't sound very loyal," Snugg growled.

Randolph laughed. "Good! That means I'm a good liar, not a bad person. Please, let me take you to lunch. By the time we're done eating you'll know whose side I'm on."

Kira nodded.

"Excellent," Randolph said. Then he turned and led the others out of the sheriff's office and into the sunlight of the early afternoon.

They walked together up the dirt road and turned left. Then, halfway down the next avenue, Mayor Randolph stopped in front of a wooden building. It was two stories tall with a balcony around the second floor. He pulled open the door and motioned for the others to step inside.

Kira was the first one to enter. As soon as she stepped inside, she could see a large open room with half a dozen tables spread over the floor, and at the back of the inn she could see a long bar lined by a dozen stools.

It all reminded Kira of the diner back home, the Silver Pancake. Her parents would take her there for breakfast on Saturday mornings or to get milkshakes on a Friday night. The only difference was that the Silver Pancake was always bright inside—even late on a Friday night—and the inn was dark and dusky inside, with deep shadows filling every corner.

Behind the bar, Kira could see a stout man with a bristly, brown beard. He was wiping a glass with a rag, and as she stepped inside, he looked up and smiled.

"Good afternoon, Samuel," the mayor call out from behind her. "If you don't mind, we'll take these two tables here. And water for everyone."

Samuel nodded his head. "As you say, sir."

Kira sat down, and Mayor Randolph took the chair closest to her. Her friends filled in the other seats at the table, and Kira tried her best to smile. There was nothing specific that she could put her finger on—the inn and Mayor Randolph both seemed normal enough—but somehow it all worked together to make Kira feel ill at ease.

Samuel arrived at the table carrying a tray filled with glasses of water. He placed one glass in front of each person. Then he reached inside the pocket of his apron for a pencil and paper.

Mayor Randolph looked up and smiled. "What are the choices today?"

Kira's mind flashed back to the menu at the Silver Pancake. Maybe just like the diner, they would serve waffles for lunch. Or maybe chicken fingers. Or milkshakes!

Samuel scratched the top of his head. "Well, I just baked a fresh liver pie this morning. Or I've got the cold haggis from yesterday. Or you could get a turkey leg. You can always have a turkey leg."

Kira felt her stomach turn. None of those choices sounded good to her. She had only tried liver once—she hated it—and the idea of sticking it inside the crust of a pie didn't sound any better. She had never even heard of haggis before, but the name itself reminded her of the exact opposite of a milkshake—and cold, leftover haggis sounded even worse. So instead, Kira ordered the turkey leg. It was the closest thing she could get to a chicken finger. Everyone else ordered the same—except for Fred, who asked for a salad and Mayor Randolph who said he preferred the cold haggis.

Mayor Randolph leaned back in his chair. "Now, Princess Kira, maybe you can tell me what you and your friends are doing in Stony Pointe."

"It's my father," Kira said, looking down at her water glass. "The Rat Queen is holding him prisoner. We've come here to save him."

Randolph pulled his hand through his gray beard. "I'm sorry to hear that, Princess. Of course, by now you've all heard the rumors. I can tell you, as someone who's spoken to the Rat Queen, it's true. She *is* crazy… and she's dangerous. If the Rat Queen truly has your father, you're right to be worried."

Kira's stomach dropped. It was exactly what she had been telling herself for the last three days, but hearing it now, spelled out so clearly by someone who actually knew the Rat Queen, made everything worse.

Mayor Randolph sat forward in his chair. "But maybe I can help. Tomorrow, I can try to take Kira to the Rat Fort—alone. The Rat Queen trusts me. If she sees it's just me and a girl, she should allow the two of us inside her castle. Then we can talk to the queen together. Maybe we can convince her to release Kira's father. What do you say?"

The more Randolph explained his plan, the more Kira felt her stomach twist into a knot. She started to shake her head, but before she could speak, Snugg answered for her.

"That's a brilliant idea, Mayor Randolph," the teddy bear growled. "We would stand forever in your debt."

Kira shot a quick look at Snugg, but the bear squeezed her hand under the table—a secret signal to stay quiet. Instead, she turned back to Randolph and forced a smile.

The mayor dabbed at his mouth with his napkin. "Think nothing of it—nothing at all. I told you I would prove my loyalty to the Rainbow family, and so I have. Now, if Princess Kira will meet me here tomorrow, at noon—alone—we can put this unpleasant business with her father to an end."

Kira stood up from the table and bowed. "Thank you, Mayor Randolph, for all that you've done." Then she led her friends out of the inn and back into the afternoon sun.

Kira was glad to be outside again, away from the mayor and the shadows of the inn. It felt like she was free. It felt like she was safe.

She turned back to look at Snugg. "I don't understand. Why would you ever agree—"

"Not here, Princess," Fred cut her off with a sharp whisper. Then he looked over his shoulder. Kira looked too. All around them, the street appeared deserted.

Even so, Fred turned back to Kira and whispered again, "We can't talk yet. Not here."

Then the zombie fixed a fake smile on his face, and he raised his voice so that he was almost shouting. "Come along, Princess. I'll lead the way back to Chloe's farm. We should get started at once."

Fred turned and started through the streets of Stony Pointe, winding his way between the buildings. He was moving even quicker than Kira expected, and at first, it was difficult for her to keep up. Every dozen steps she found herself running to catch up with the zombie. Chloe and Ben had to do the same. Only Snugg was able to match Fred's speed, but the tiny bear stayed at the rear of their column, making sure no one fell too far behind.

It wasn't until they cleared the last of the houses that Kira noticed Fred's hand resting on the handle of his sword, ready to draw the weapon at a moment's notice. Apparently they weren't as free or as safe as Kira had thought.

Finally, Fred stopped on the hill overlooking the tiny town; he turned back to Kira. "Now, Princess, what were you trying to say before?"

"Why—" Kira struggled to catch her breath. "Why did we run away from the village?"

"We weren't safe there," Fred answered, letting go of his sword. "I don't trust Mayor Randolph."

"Neither do I," Snugg growled.

"Well neither do I," Kira said, throwing up her hands. "But that's my other question. Why would you send me with him alone tomorrow?"

"That was a lie, Princess." Snugg shook his head, rubbing his tiny paw back and forth over his chin. "You won't be meeting anyone tomorrow. You won't need to, because we're saving your dad tonight."

Chapter 8: Water Rat Bay

Kira's heart was racing. "What do you mean, 'tonight'?"

It was exactly what she wanted to hear—ever since she learned that her father was sold to the Rat Queen, Kira dreamed of rescuing him, and now it was finally happening. She was excited to see him and scared she might fail, but more than either of those, Kira felt ready.

She looked at Snugg. "You really think we can save my dad tonight?"

Snugg rubbed his chin. "I think we *have* to save your dad tonight, before Mayor Randolph can betray us to the Rat Queen or Pike. We can't wait any longer."

"Well I think you're crazy." Chloe crossed her arms. "There's no way y'all can get inside her castle. That thing's a fortress."

Snugg nodded. "That's exactly what it is. And do you know what that fortress is called?"

Chloe nodded. "It's called the Rat Fort."

Snugg pointed his paw out to the ocean. Everyone looked. In the distance, Kira could see the black stone walls of the Rat Fort rising above the water, cutting against the blue sky.

"And where does the Rat Fort sit?" Snugg growled.

Chloe shrugged. "Out in the middle of Water Rat Bay. Why does that matter?"

"Water Rat Bay!" Ben shouted. "Of course it matters! I didn't even think about that before."

Chloe shook her head. "I still don't understand."

Kira tried to remember. Ben, Fred, and Snugg had all spoken about Water Rat Bay in the past. Kira knew it was the name of a battle in the Zombie War.

She also knew it was where Snugg earned his nickname "The Destroyer." Other than that, everything about Water Rat Bay remained a mystery, and Kira was tired of being left in the dark.

She looked at the teddy bear. "Why is Water Rat Bay so important, Snugg? What happened there?"

Snugg shook his head. "It doesn't matter, Princess. It all happened a long time ago."

"It *does* matter!" Kira shouted back. "If I'm going to be a princess in this world, then I have a right to know."

Fred lowered his eyes. "That's true, Princess, but it's not something we like to talk about."

"Not on either side," Snugg added. "No one who was there likes to talk about it."

For a second, Kira felt a pang of disappointment. Whatever happened at Water Rat Bay must have been painful—for everyone—but that only made her question more important.

Then Ben cleared his throat. He looked back and forth between Fred and Snugg. "I can tell her the story, if you want. I wasn't at the battle, but I know what I've read and what I've been told."

Fred nodded. "Then you should be the one to tell her. The princess is right, she deserves to know the truth."

Ben closed his eyes. "It all started when Bill became King of the Zombies. The first thing he did was gather his army. Then he declared war on the Rainbow King. Everyone thought it was a joke at first."

Kira's face twisted. "Why? Why would people think war was a joke?"

"Because no one had declared war in the kingdoms for over a hundred years," Snugg growled. "When it finally happened, no one was ready for it."

Ben opened his eyes to stare at the Rat Fort. "The Rainbow King's army was much stronger than the Zombies, but they were divided. There were soldiers in the East, more soldiers in the West, and still more in the North. They were spread out to defend *all* the kingdoms."

"And that's what they were supposed to do: protect the kingdoms." Fred shook his head, taking up the story. "But Bill understood their weakness. The Rainbow Army was parceled out between the kingdoms, and it would take time to gather their reinforcements. If Bill could keep his army together—if he could move quickly enough—he could take the capitol city and the Rainbow Throne before anyone could move to stop him."

Ben kicked his foot through the tall grass. "So no one paid much attention when Bill marched his army east into the Nightmare Lands. The zombies had been fighting battles there for years. Everyone assumed it was just a new king showing off for his people. But then Bill turned his army north, and in November, he met the Rainbow Army of the East in a field near the village of Mareritt."

Ben stopped himself and looked up, meeting Kira's eyes. She could tell by the look on his face—his eyebrows pinched together—that it was difficult for him to tell this story. But that only made the story that much more important.

"What happened next?" Kira asked.

Ben took a deep breath. "The Army of the East lost, and they lost badly. They were driven from the field. And no one saw it coming."

"No one except King Bill," Fred added, turning his back to the ocean and the Rat Fort. "Beating the Army of the East was *exactly* what Bill expected—what he wanted."

"I was a young bear serving in the Army of the West," Snugg growled, staring down at his feet. "When we heard the news of the battle, we all understood what it meant. No one stood between the zombies and the Rainbow City. The King and all of the kingdoms would be lost. And so that night, I took a suggestion to our commander—"

"It was more than a suggestion," Ben said. "I've read all about it, Snugg. You took General Hornraven a plan to save the world—"

Snugg shook his head. "It was only an idea, Ben. Trust me. And it was a desperate idea, at that. I told the general we should attack the Zombie Kingdom from the west."

Kira's nose wrinkled. "But how would attacking the Zombie Kingdom save the Rainbow City?"

"Because zombies are loyal," Fred answered, looking at Kira. "We're famous for it. 'Zombie loyalty' they call it. It's the reason I fought with the Zombies against Snugg in the war, and it's the reason Snugg's plan would work. You see, when Bill declared war on the Rainbow Kingdom, he had to take the entire army with him if he was going to have a chance to win—everyone who was old enough and strong enough to carry a sword was gone. So if our kingdom was ever attacked, Bill would need to return with his army to defend our homes… because of Zombie loyalty."

"Only he didn't take *all* of the zombies," Ben said, looking at Fred. "He left three hundred of his best soldiers behind to guard Water Rat Bay. King Bill realized the only way to attack the Zombie Kingdom from the west was to pass through the bay. If an army passed any farther north, they would need to march over the Gryphon Mountains, and that would take far too long."

Just hearing the name—Water Rat Bay—sent a current of electricity down Kira's spine. This was what she had been waiting for, what she needed to know. "And what happened at Water Rat Bay?"

Fred looked down at his hands. "Water Rat Bay is guarded by the Rat Fort. It sits on an island in the middle of the water, with its towering black stone walls rising straight up from the water. At each of its four corners, sitting on top of the four towers, there stands a trebuchet."

Kira was confused. "What's a… a… treb-u-something?"

"TREB. YOO. SHAY." Ben sounded out the word for her. "It's like a catapult, only it uses a counterweight. The trebuchets on the Rat Fort are famous in our world."

Fred continued, but now his voice sounded distant, like he was really talking to himself. "Those trebuchets controlled the entire beach. They controlled the water. No one could stand and fight within range of those trebuchets. And so we thought we were safe."

Snugg shook his head. "But there's a secret way into the fort, Princess. A hidden tunnel at the back of the island. You can't even see it unless it's low tide. Otherwise it's covered by the water. That night, before the battle, I used the tunnel to lead a team of soldiers inside the fort. We snuck past the guards to the tops of the four towers, and we sabotaged the trebuchets. We jammed the releases so they couldn't fire. And then we waited."

"On the morning of the battle," Fred said, his voice still low, "the zombies in the fort marched onto the bridge connecting the Rat Fort to the mainland. Our only job was to keep the fighting on the beach, because if their army moved too close to the fort, the trebuchets would be useless. But as the battle started, and their army charged the fort, we knew right away that something was wrong. The trebuchets kept silent. They didn't throw a single stone. That's when we tried to retreat inside the fort—"

"But we lowered the portcullis behind them," Snugg growled. "They were trapped on the bridge."

Then, for a moment, there was silence. Everyone stopped talking, and it was like no one wanted to finish the story. Kira looked back and forth between Snugg and Fred, waiting for one of them to speak first, but neither did.

Finally, Ben's voice fell to a whisper. "At the start of the battle, three hundred zombies defended the Rat Fort. When the fighting was over, only eighteen were left, taken as prisoners."

"Including me," Fred said, forcing a thin smile. "I told you, Princess, that Zombies are loyal, and so we were. We were all there fighting for our homes out of loyalty. And then, at the end, we were fighting for each other. They were brave zombies in the Rat Fort, Princess, every last one of them… and they were my friends."

Then Kira felt cold inside. It was like she heard a story that she was never meant to know. She wished she could go back and never ask her stupid question. There was so much pain, even in just listening to the story.

She tried to say, “I’m sorry,” but the words caught in her throat.

Snugg stepped closer to Kira, reaching up and taking her hand. “Now there’s just one more question you need to ask, Princess—the last part of the story. Do you have it?”

Kira tried to remember everything they told her, everything about King Bill, and the armies, and the attack on the Rat Fort… and then she knew the question, but she also knew the answer.

She looked down at Snugg. “How did you know about the tunnel?”

Then Snugg stood up straight, like he was a soldier standing at attention, and he raised his chin. Kira thought his voice sounded strange, as if it took all his strength to say the words. “I knew about the tunnel because my friend told me about it. He told me when we were still children, years before the battle—long before King Bill, or the Zombie War, or Water Rat Bay ever happened. He told me *because* we were friends, and what happened there—the massacre at Water Rat Bay—it’s not his fault.”

Kira looked in the same direction that Snugg was staring, and she could see Fred standing alone.

Kira shook her head. "And that's why you were exiled? Because Snugg knew about that tunnel? That was the reason?"

Fred nodded. "One of many, I'm afraid. But my exile… it wasn't Snugg's fault, either. And he needs to understand that. I don't blame him."

Then Kira could feel her eyes filling with warm tears as everything blurred. She wanted to say something. She wanted to apologize or explain why everything would be okay, but she knew deep inside there was nothing to say. It wasn't her story to fix. She could only listen and share in their sadness.

Then Fred stepped forward, and Snugg ran to meet him. The two friends hugged. Then Kira couldn't hold back anymore. She ran up and squeezed both of them with the biggest hug she could manage, her sad and happy tears running together.

Chapter 9: Caught in the Dark

"So is that your plan?" Ben asked, looking at the bear. "You want us to use the secret tunnel to sneak into the Rat Fort?"

"That's the best plan we've got," Snugg growled. "We'll wait for night and low tide. Then we'll steal a boat and rescue Kira's father."

"And what should I do?" Chloe asked, stepping closer to stand next to Kira. "Should I go with you? You want me to find the boat?"

"The best thing you can do is to go back to your grandpa's farm," Fred answered.

Snugg nodded. “Fred’s right. Go home, lock your doors, and stay inside. If everything works, we’ll see you in the morning… along with Kira’s dad.”

“Absolutely not,” Chloe stamped her foot to the ground. “I promised Kira I would help rescue her dad. We made a deal.”

Kira put her hand on the girl’s shoulder and smiled. “When we rescue my dad, we’re going to need some place to hide—especially if Pike and the Rat Queen are after us. Fred and Snugg are right: the best way you can help is by letting us hide at your farm.”

Chloe frowned and turned to Kira. “Then I guess I’ll see you in the morning. We got a deal?”

Kira smiled. “Deal.”

Then Chloe started up the hill, toward the forest and her grandpa’s farm, and there was nothing for the others to do except wait.

Kira sat down on the soft grass looking out over the gray water and the black walls of the Rat Fort. It was still another hour before the sun would set, and she didn't know how much longer it would take after that for low tide to reveal the secret door.

Kira tried to imagine where inside the castle the Rat Queen was holding her father. Would he be locked away in the basement, chained up inside some dark dungeon? Or would she keep him inside one of the towers?

Snugg's rescue plan sounded simple enough. The village of Stony Pointe was right on the water's edge, so it would be easy enough to steal a boat. Fred and Snugg both knew about the secret tunnel, so there should be no problem finding it once they got to the far side of the Rat Fort. All that remained was finding Kira's dad and escaping before the Rat Queen realized he was missing. It all gave Kira hope that their plan might actually work.

Finally, as the sun dipped below the Gryphon Mountains in the west, Snugg rose to his feet. "It's time."

The tiny, stuffed bear started down the hill, and Kira, Fred, and Ben all followed, moving silently between the shadows. They stayed on the outside of the town, crouching against the walls of the buildings and darting between alleys where they might be seen. Finally, they reached the edge of the water.

Snugg raised his paw and whispered. "You wait here. I'll be right back."

Then the little bear ran away. Kira tried to watch him go, but it was already too dark—after a couple of steps, Snugg's dark brown fur was lost in the shadows.

Kira tried to listen instead. At first, all she could hear were the small waves breaking over the rocks on the shore, but then she heard another sound—footsteps—and they were getting closer.

She turned around to face Fred and Ben, ready to tell them that they were discovered, but before she could speak, Snugg emerged from the shadows. It was his footsteps they'd heard.

He waved his arm at the others. "This way."

Kira followed Snugg along the shoreline, until finally the bear turned to his left and started down a wooden pier. At the end of the dock, Kira could see a small rowboat bobbing up and down in the waves.

“Here we are,” Snugg said. “Everyone climb in.”

Kira obeyed at once, taking her seat in the bow of the boat. Fred and Ben both followed, sitting down in the middle. Then Snugg untied the ropes holding the small rowboat in place, and he jumped into the stern.

Fred and Ben each took one of the oars at the side of the boat, and with every stroke, the sheer black walls of the fortress loomed higher and higher before them. Snugg turned the rudder at the back, and the tiny rowboat skirted left, hugging the rocky shore of the island until finally they were on the far side of the fortress.

“Can you see it?” Snugg whispered from the back of the boat.

“No. I think it may be farther around… No! I see it. There it is.” Fred pointed straight toward the island.

Kira leaned forward, trying to see, but everything was too dark. The sky, the Rat Fort, the stones, the water—it all looked like different shades of black ink running together on a piece of black paper. She looked again, trying to focus exactly where Fred was pointing.

Then she could see it, too: a small, round grate just above the waterline, hidden between the rocks. It looked like it was made from rusted metal, and it wasn't much bigger than a car tire, but Kira could definitely see it now. That was the way to her father.

Ben pulled on his oar. Fred did the same, and the tiny boat bumped forward against the rocks of the island.

"Grab that boulder. Pull us in closer." Snugg gave the orders as he looped a rope around another rock, tying the boat to the shore.

Then Fred took hold of the grate and pulled. Nothing happened. He pulled again, and Kira could hear the high-pitched shriek of metal scraping against metal. Now Ben took hold of the grate too, and they pulled together. The grating popped free and fell into the bottom of the rowboat. Kira looked at the open mouth of the pipe, but it was far too dark to see inside.

Snugg stepped into the middle of the boat. “I’ll go first, Princess, but I want you to stay right behind me.” Then the tiny bear hopped into the pipe.

Kira followed. Inside the pipe it was just as dark as it looked from the outside. It was impossible to see anything—even Snugg. It made the pipe feel even more cramped then it already was. Kira crawled forward on her hands and knees, her shoulders squeezing against the curved walls of the pipe. Everywhere her skin touched, it felt cold, wet, and slimy. Kira imagined thick green algae lining every inch of the metal tunnel, and just the picture in her head made her gag. *Maybe it was better that she couldn’t see.*

“Woah!” Kira heard Snugg’s voice cry out in front of her, so loud it startled her.

“Snugg?” Kira whispered. Then she crawled forward again. Before she even realized what was happening, Kira’s hand touched nothing but air. The pipe had ended. She was falling now—only a couple of feet. She landed on a hard, stone floor.

Kira scrambled back to her feet just in time. No sooner did she stand up than another dull thud came from behind her, and she heard Ben's voice. "Uff."

Then another dull thud—softer than the one before—but she heard Ben's voice again, louder this time. "Oof."

Ben must have been slower to get up than Kira, because that second "thud" was Fred. The zombie landed on top of him—at least that's what Kira imagined. It was still impossible to see anything. Kira strained her eyes and reached out with both of her hands, but she touched nothing. Wherever they were now, it was bigger than the pipe. That was the only thing Kira knew for certain.

"Where are we?" Snugg growled in the dark.

"I'm not sure. Should be the dungeon, I think," Fred answered.

"Why's it so dark?" Snugg growled again.

"I-I'm not sure. I thought there would be torches burning or something."

Kira felt her heart sink into her stomach. The whole plan depended on finding her father quickly and escaping before they were discovered.

"We need to find some light or none of this will work," she said. "Ben, can you try to make—"

"I already told you, Kira, I can't build anything with the light."

"That's not true," Kira said. "You said you can make a ball of light. Right now, that's all we need."

"I don't think I can."

"Right now we just need you to try," Kira said.

"This isn't going to work," the boy grumbled.

Kira looked in the direction of Ben's voice. Then, to her surprise, she could actually see something. At first it looked like a pair of hands folded together, but the skin was colored a deep red. It reminded Kira of the way her own hands looked when she held them over a flashlight.

Then the hands opened, and Kira could see they belonged to Ben. She could see his face too. It was lit by a warm glow—a dancing light like the flame in an oil lamp—and resting inside the palms of his hands, she could see an orb of yellow light no bigger than a tennis ball.

Kira laughed. “Ben, that’s— That’s amazing.”

Ben stared down at the orb resting in his hands. “Not really. I already told you, anyone can do this much.”

Kira shook her head. “Not anyone. I know I can’t.”

Suddenly, she had a hundred questions for Ben about how to shape the light, but before she could ask any of them, Snugg’s low growl stopped her.

“Princess.”

The bear’s voice sounded strange—strange, but familiar. Something was wrong. Then Kira remembered that Snugg had sounded like this before—at her house with the zombies. The tiny bear was ready for a fight.

Kira wheeled around, and then she could see the danger for herself. All around them, the floor was moving, bobbing up and down like the small waves of the ocean, only it wasn’t covered by water—it was covered by fur. A thousand rats filled the room, and they were all facing the four companions.

Then a door opened, and the dark silhouette of a girl filled the doorway, pointing a long finger down at the friends.

She shouted, "Get them!"

Then the rats rushed forward.

Chapter 10: The Queen of the Rats

Kira sat against the stone wall, iron manacles clamped around both of her wrists with heavy chains stretching behind her, reaching over her head, and anchoring her to the wall.

Snugg was chained next to her, a single rusted shackle fastened around his neck. The bear's head drooped forward, and Kira could see that his eyes were open, staring at the floor, but he didn't speak.

On her other side, she could see Fred, and farther away she could see Ben, both of them sitting against the wall, chained by their wrists.

Kira shook her head. She still couldn't believe that everything went wrong so quickly. She remembered the door opening and the shadowed figure of a girl giving the command, "Get them."

Then everything happened at once. The army of rats ran forward. Kira remembered their fur brushing past her feet and the pin-prick of their claws as the rats climbed up her jeans and onto her shirt. Then she lost her balance and fell backwards, but she didn't hit the stone floor. She landed on a soft bed of rats, as if they were ready to catch her. Then they swarmed over top of her, covering her face so that she couldn't see—and for a second, she couldn't breathe—but then the rats ran away. They left the room completely.

Kira remembered how she thought she was free, but as she sat up from the floor, she found the iron chains bound to her wrists. The rats had done it—they had chained her to the wall—and now she was a prisoner of the Rat Queen. Kira shivered at the memory, and the thought of being someone's prisoner again.

She rose to her feet. “So what do we do now?”

“What do you mean?” Ben asked, pulling hard against his chains so that the metal links rattled through the empty room. “We’re captured. There’s nothing we can do.”

“That’s not good enough. We can’t just give up.” Kira looked at Ben. “Maybe you can use the light to build us a key?”

Ben shook his head. “I can’t do that. I told you—”

“But you can try.” Kira pressed. “Or you can use the light to make a hammer. Then we can break the chains—”

“It won’t work, Princess.” Fred forced a smile. “Even if Ben could make a hammer, these chains are much too strong.” Then, to prove his point, Fred pulled hard against the chains, just like Ben, and the sound of rattling metal echoed in the room.

“Well, I’m not giving up.” Kira took a deep breath, and with all her strength, she lunged forward, throwing the full weight of her body against the chains, and all at once, the manacles popped open and Kira spilled onto the floor.

"It worked!" Ben shouted.

Fred scrambled to his feet. "The rats must have made a mistake. They never set your locks, Princess. You were free from the start."

Kira picked herself up from the ground and brushed the dirt from her jeans. "Now what do I do?"

"You leave," Snugg growled. "Get back to the boat and escape."

"I'm not going to leave you." Kira reached for the handle of her sword.

Snugg shook his head. "You can't fix this problem, Princess. You need to escape."

Kira looked down at her hand, clutching the handle of her rapier, ready to draw the blade, but she remembered what her father said. Using her sword wouldn't help. She needed to be smarter, braver, and kinder—something much more difficult.

Kira let go of her rapier and unbuckled her belt, letting it fall to the floor.

"What are you doing?" Snugg growled.

"I'm going to talk to the Rat Queen, and I'm going to save us… All of us."

Fred shook his head. "Then take your sword, Princess. Better to have a sword and not need it than need a sword and not have it."

Kira smiled. "You're usually right, Fred, but not this time. Swords won't fix this problem." Kira turned and started up the stairs from the dungeon. The door at the top of the steps was still open.

Snugg shouted after her. "You should leave us, Princess! Escape while you can."

Kira turned back to look down at her friends. "I can't do that, Snugg. I need to try." Then she stepped through the open door.

The hallway beyond the dungeon was nothing like she expected. The dungeon itself was cold, damp, and dark with black stone walls and floors. The hallway felt like the opposite. It was warm and inviting, with white paneled walls, a deep burgundy carpet, and a hundred candles lighting the corridor.

Kira tried to think about what she might say to the Rat Queen, what argument would convince her to let Kira's friends and father leave the castle unharmed, but nothing seemed good enough. Every conversation she imagined ended with the Rat Queen laughing at her and throwing her back in the dungeon. Then a new thought crept inside Kira's head. *How would she ever find the Rat Queen in this castle?*

"Hello there," a loud voice said behind her.

Kira jumped in her own skin and spun around, her heart racing inside her chest. The last thing she expected was to hear a voice in the hallway—especially a voice so close behind her—but now, standing just a couple of feet away, Kira saw a girl.

The girl was taller than Kira, but she looked about the same age. She wore a simple blue dress with a white belt tied around her waist, and a pair of faded jeans underneath. The outfit was finished with a pair of black canvas sneakers.

Kira thought the girl was pretty. She had a friendly smile and pale green eyes. In fact, the only thing out of place was the girl's hair. Her long, dark hair was twisted and knotty, with stray tendrils flying out in a thousand directions.

Kira's nose wrinkled. "Who are you?"

The girl clapped her hands, and jumped into the air. "Oooh! This is perfect! I *love* guessing games—"

Then, just as quickly as her excitement started, it seemed to sour, and the girl's smiling face turned into a frown. "But I suppose it's not a very *good* game. You see, I already know who I am, so I suppose I already win."

"Oh." Kira shook her head. "That's not actually— What I meant to say is— I mean… Who *are* you?"

"I'm Sarah, of course." The girl smiled again. "I spell it with an 'H', but the 'H' is silent. Can you spell it? My name, I mean. Not the word 'it.'"

Kira nodded. "I think so. S-A-R-A-H. Is that right?"

Sarah clapped her hands. "That's perfect. You're very good at this, you know. Of course, sometimes I spell my name with the 'H' in the middle, and other times I spell it with the 'H' at the very start. You see, it doesn't really matter, because the 'H' is silent. Other times I make the 'H' invisible all together, and then no one even knows it's there. What's your name?"

Kira felt like she was going to be dizzy. The girl talked very fast, and even though all her words made sense, it was difficult to follow what she was saying. Kira shook her head again. "My name is Kira, I guess."

"Kira-I-guess." Sarah laughed, running all the sounds together into a single word. "That's a funny name for a girl."

"No. It's just Kira. My name is Kira."

"Tell me, Kira, do you spell your name with an 'H'?" Sarah reached out, taking hold of both of Kira's hands.

"No. There's no 'H'. It's just K-I-R-A."

"That's too bad." Sarah sucked in a quick breath of air between her teeth. "Maybe your 'H' is invisible, like mine, and no one ever told you about it."

Kira pulled back her hands. She was feeling frustrated now. She needed to find the Rat Queen, not play games with some silly girl wandering around the halls of the castle.

"Why are you even here?" Kira asked.

"Oh, that's a much better question!" Sarah looked up at the ceiling. "It's like… the meaning of life. Why are *any* of us here?"

"No. That's not what I mean. I mean—"

Sarah looked again at Kira. "You mean why am I *here*?" Sarah pointed down at the floor. "You're asking why am I in the Rat Fort. It's because I live here. Because I own it. Because it's mine. I'm the Rat Queen, I think… Or am I the Queen of the Rats? I can never decide which one sounds better. What do you think, Kira?"

Kira's stomach twisted into a pretzel. "You mean you're the Rat Queen?"

"I guess I am. Although, I *do* like the sound of the other one… 'Queen of the Rats.' Maybe I should just use both." Sarah pulled out the hem of her dress and curtseyed in front of Kira. "I'm Sarah the Rat Queen,

Queen of the Rats. What do you think? Is it too much?"

Kira staggered back. "But—but you don't even *look* like a rat!"

Sarah turned her head to the side. "That's so sweet—so very nice of you to say. And I don't think you look anything like a dolphin."

Then Sarah clapped her hands and jumped into the air. "That was fun. I like this game much better than your first game. Let's do it again. I'll go first this time. You don't look anything like a… like a… like a buffalo."

Kira stamped her foot down on the carpet. "You're not listening! You had me locked up in chains."

Sarah nodded. "Oh, I know. Wasn't it terrible?"

"And you ordered your rats to attack me!"

Sarah nodded again. "I remember. That's how you got put in chains in the first place, but I told my rats not to actually lock the manacles so that you could escape. And you did, because here you are!"

Kira's face flushed red—she was angry now. "You're the one holding my father prisoner!"

Sarah cringed. "I am? I'm so sorry. I didn't know that. Which one's your father? Is he the bear or the zombie?"

"He's neither! He's—" Kira stopped herself mid-sentence. She closed her eyes and took a deep breath. Then, when she started again, her voice was slow and measured. "My name is Princess Kira the First, Defender of the Kingdoms, Lady of the Unicorn Spire, Queen of the Zombies, and Heiress to the Rainbow Throne. I want my father back."

Then Sarah's mouth dropped open. "Kira! Do you know what this means? It means we're sisters!"

Kira staggered back. "What?"

Chapter 11: Fromage de Rongeur

Kira stared straight ahead. "What do you mean we're sisters? That's impossible. Both of my parents were exiled a long time ago—before I was ever born."

"Well, we're not really sisters, silly." Sarah laughed. "But we *are* cousins, and I don't have any other cousins, so that means we're more like sisters than cousins. And I don't have any *real* sisters either, so that makes you absolutely perfect! We'll be best-friend-sister-cousins, forever!"

Sarah threw her arms around Kira, squeezing her so tight that Kira couldn't breathe.

"Sarah, wait. You need to let me go." Kira wiggled free from the girl's embrace. "You need to explain all of this. How—how are we cousins?"

"Well, it's simple, really. You start with seven sisters: Scarlet, Saphron, Daisy, Aileen, Odele, Indigo, and Violet." Sarah counted off each one on her fingers as she recited their names.

"Wait a minute." Kira shook her head. "You mean to say that I have *seven* aunts?"

Sarah smiled. "Well, no, silly. You really only have six, because your mom is Aunt Scarlet, so she can't be your aunt. She was always my favorite, you know—"

"That's impossible. You don't even know my mom," Kira said.

"Oh, I know I don't. She's so mysterious that way. Of course that's just like Aunt Scarlet—mysterious, I mean. Are you mysterious too?"

Kira didn't feel mysterious. In fact, since the moment she met Sarah, she mostly felt confused. She started to shake her head.

"Oh, it doesn't matter," Sarah interrupted her. "I'm not mysterious either. Maybe that's why I don't have any friends. People think I'm crazy, you know. It's probably because I say what I think as soon as I think it. There's no mystery in that at all, but does that sound crazy to you? Like your hair.'"

"What?" Both of Kira's hands flew to her head, trying to hide as much of her pink hair as possible. She suddenly felt like she was back in her own world, riding the bus to school with Sophia. In fact, she was certain that the very next words out of Sarah's mouth would be something about "Kira the Weird."

But instead, Sarah pulled away Kira's hands. Then she reached for Kira's hair, letting the locks of neon pink cascade between her fingers. "I mean I *like* your hair. I think it's beautiful. I wish I could have hair like yours. Do you mind?"

Kira felt her face flush warm, and she knew she must be blushing. "No, I don't mind."

"That's perfect," Sarah raised her voice, "Chase!"

Just then, a pointy, white-furred nose jabbed out of the middle of Sarah's tangled hair. It wiggled back and forth, sniffing the air. Then it poked forward again, and Kira could see the nose belonged to a rat. She could see its big, round ears and its tiny, black eyes, and its long, square teeth jutting down from its mouth.

Kira jumped back. "Sarah, you—you have a rat in your hair."

"Oh, I know that." Sarah looked straight up with her eyes, trying to see past her own forehead to catch a glimpse of the rat. "That's Chase. He's my royal seneschal It means he's my second in command. He lives up there."

Kira shook her head. "He lives in your hair?"

"Well, of course he does. I mean, we all have to live somewhere, right?"

Kira was still shaking her head. She wanted to say something else—to explain to Sarah why rats shouldn't live in your hair—but every time she started to think of a reason, it wouldn't quite make sense. After all, Sarah had a point: we all have to live somewhere.

Kira was still thinking when Chase the rat started to squeak.

"I'm sorry about that, but something else came up," Sarah said out loud, and Kira thought the words were meant for the rat.

Chase squeaked again, rising up on his hind legs on top of Sarah's head.

"Yes, I know when you take your naps, but this is much more important."

Chase squeaked again.

Sarah nodded. "That's right. My favorite cousin said I could have her hair. Would you mind getting the scissors and the tape?"

Kira's stomach twisted at thought of having her hair chopped off by a rat. "No, Sarah, you misunderstood. That's not going to work."

"Oh! I guess I didn't think about that." Sarah looked up again, trying to see the rat sitting on top of her head. "Princess Kira is absolutely right—tape will never work. We're going to need the glue—lots of glue. What was I even thinking? I can't just tape her hair to my head."

"No!" Kira shouted. Then she caught herself, took a slow breath, and started again. "What I meant to say is that I would much prefer it if you *didn't* cut my hair."

"Well, then, of course we won't, silly. Why didn't you just say so from the beginning? I mean, it is *your* hair after all. But if we're not going to give you a haircut, then what would you like to do instead? Maybe you want to see where your father is."

Kira's heart jumped into her throat; it was difficult to speak. "Oh, yes. I would love that."

"Perfect." Sarah looked straight up and started to make squeaking sounds like a rat.

Then Chase jumped off her head, landed heavy on the ground, and scurried down the hall. Kira tried to watch the rat as he ran, but then he darted to the left, slipped through a large crack in the wall, and he was gone.

Sarah took Kira by the arm and led her slowly down the hall, walking in the same direction as Chase. "I sent him ahead of us to get the others ready for our tour. I have so many places to show you. You're going to love it."

"Is that what you were doing?" Kira asked. "I only heard you squeaking. Can you actually talk to the rats? Can they understand what you say?"

Sarah stopped at the door at the end of the hall. "That's a more difficult question than you would think. You see, animals can *always* understand what we say. They understand you, me, and everyone else. They're so much smarter than us in that regard. The problem is we can't understand them, or talk back in their own language—maybe because we don't like to listen. That's why I use magic instead."

"You can do magic?"

Sarah nodded. "It's called the Indigo Animal spell, and I learned it from my mom. It's amazing. It's the reason I can understand my rats. I'd be lost without it. But what about you? Can you do any magic?"

"Actually, I can," Kira said. Only a few days ago, her answer would have been no. Kira never felt like a magical person, but that was before she met Snugg,

Ben, and Fred, and it was before she learned the Purple Butterfly spell.

Kira said the words, “Flutter-by-us. Butterfly-with-us.”

Then she felt a strange tickle between her shoulder blades, like when you have an itch that you can never scratch. She saw a flash of purple out of the corner of her eye, and she knew that the purple butterfly wings were stretching out on either side of her shoulders. Then Kira’s feet lifted off the ground, and she was floating in mid-air.

“That’s incredible!” Sarah shouted. “Just like Aunt Violet. You’re amazing!”

Kira closed her eyes and dropped to the ground. Her face felt warm, and she knew she was blushing. “I’m not, really. I mean, it’s nothing special. It’s just—”

“Of course it’s special!” Sarah grabbed both of Kira’s hands. “I’ve always wanted to fly, but purple magic doesn’t work for me.”

Then Sarah’s eyes opened wide, and she started jumping up and down. “Try my spell. Try the Indigo

Animal spell. Maybe you can do that one, too" Sarah stopped herself from jumping and stood rigid straight, trying to be serious. "Repeat after me: Squeak. Squawk."

Kira repeated. "Squeak. Squawk."

Sarah clapped her hands. "Perfect. Next you say the name of an animal you want to talk to. So say, 'Rats.'"

Kira nodded. "Rats."

"That's great." Sarah clapped again. "Now just say the word, 'Talk' and you're done."

"Talk," Kira said.

"Now put it all together. Say it fast."

"Squeak. Squawk. Rats. Talk." Kira looked around the empty hall, not sure what to do next. She certainly didn't *feel* any different, like she did with her butterfly wings. She turned to Sarah. "Did it work?"

Sarah shrugged. "I have no idea." Then she called out in a louder voice. "Chase, come back here, please."

Kira looked down and saw the white rat squeeze himself through the crack in the wall. Then he ran forward to stand in front of Sarah and Kira, and he rose up on his hind legs.

Chase squeaked, "You called for me, Your Majesty?"

Kira's mouth dropped open. "I-I can understand him!" Then she pointed down at Chase. "I can understand you. Can you understand me?"

Chase looked up, his thin nose wiggling in the air. "Of course, Princess Kira. It's a pleasure to make your acquaintance."

Kira turned back to Sarah. "Can I talk in rat language now?"

"Sure," Sarah said. "Just make some squeaky noises like a rat, but think about the words you want to say. The magic will take care of the rest."

Kira gulped in a deep breath, and then she let it out with a tiny, "Squeak, squeak, squeak." But even though she heard herself squeaking, she knew what the sounds really meant.

"It's nice to meet you, too," she squeaked.

Chase the rat folded himself over at his waist, bowing to the two girls. "If it please, Your Majesties, the grand tour of the Rat Fort is ready. Shall we begin?"

"Absolutely." Sarah picked Chase up from the ground and set him on top of her shoulder. Then she pulled open the door and stepped through. Kira followed.

In the next room, the first thing Kira noticed was the smell. It was a creamy smell, like milk, mixed with a thousand other flavors—sweet, spicy, and a little stinky. Kira knew those smells as soon as they filled her nose. It was cheese.

She looked around the room and saw a dozen copper pots sitting over small fires, each one filled to the brim with milk, and she saw at least twenty wooden vats overflowing with something that looked like lumpy white and yellow goop, and all around the walls of the room, reaching all the way to the ceiling, Kira saw wooden shelves stacked high with the finished cheese. It was shaped into blocks, and wheels, and triangles, all of different sizes, filling every empty space on the shelves. And all across the floor, running between the pots and vats, and scurrying up the shelves, Kira could see hundreds of rats.

"Well, what do you think?" Sarah asked.

Kira turned around on her heels, trying to look in every corner of the room at once. "It's impressive."

"And here are my royal cheesemakers." Sarah motioned with her hand towards the ground. "They take care of everything for me, and they do such a nice job."

Kira looked down, and three rats stood on their hind legs in front of the girls.

"Kira, allow me to introduce Chef James, Chef Cole, and Chef Shane. They make the best cheeses in the world!" Sarah said.

In unison, the three rats bowed their noses to the ground. Then Chef James said, "We are at your service, Your Majesty."

"Their cheese really is delightful," Sarah said. "You should try some. We call it *Fromage de Rongeur*, but that's really just fancy words for 'Rat

Cheese.' We sell it all over the kingdoms. That's the reason why I have so much money, and I guess it's a good thing I do. Otherwise, I could never afford to feed my rats. They eat so much, you see."

Kira shook her head. "Why don't you just let them eat the cheese?"

Sarah's mouth dropped open. "Why…?" Then she looked at Chase still sitting on her shoulder. "Why didn't you think of that?"

Sarah laughed. "Oh, Kira, that's a brilliant idea. You're so smart. I'm going to make you my Grand Vizier."

Kira smiled. "What's a Grand Vizier? What would you expect me to do? I'm afraid I don't know anything about cheese."

"Well of course not, silly. As Grand Vizier you would be my advisor and my best friend. You would give me advice on everything! What do you say? Will you do it?"

Kira laughed. "I guess so."

Sarah clapped her hands and jumped into the air. "This is perfect! You just have to pass the test, and then you're hired. Are you ready?"

Kira nodded.

Then Sarah tried her best to stop smiling and look serious. "Question one—this is an easy one. Do you trust me?"

The smile slipped from Kira's face. It may have been an easy question for Sarah to ask, but not so easy for Kira to answer. Everything she heard about the Rat Queen was that she was mean and crazy. Then she met Sarah for herself, and she found that neither one of those things was true. Sarah was different, but so was Kira, and different wasn't the same as crazy. And she wasn't mean, either. That much was obvious.

Kira decided. "I do trust you, Sarah."

Sarah clapped her hands. "Excellent! That's the right answer. Now for the last question. Can *I* trust you?"

Kira smiled—this question really *was* easy. "Of course you can. Always."

"Perfect!" Sarah stuck out her arm to shake Kira's hand. "Welcome to the team, Grand Vizier. So, what should we do now?"

"Well, you mentioned seeing my dad," Kira said.

Sarah slapped her hand to her forehead. "Of course I did, silly. This way. Follow me."

Sarah walked across the cheese room to a heavy wooden door. "It's right through here."

Then she pulled back the door and stepped inside.

Kira followed, but as she stepped through the open door, she discovered the room was empty.

Chapter 12: The Throne Room

Kira looked around the room again. On the far wall there was a thin slit for a window, throwing a rectangle of sunlight across the scattered straw on the floor. Other than that, the room was empty, aside from Sarah, Chase and herself.

Kira felt her stomach tighten like she was about to get sick. She turned to Sarah and screamed, "Where's my dad? He's not here! You said you would show me my father!"

Sarah shook her head. "I never said that. I never told you Uncle Henry was *here*. I told you I would show you where he *is*, and so that's what I'm doing."

Sarah pointed to the window in the far wall. "I sent your dad west into the Gryphon Mountains. He's with my mom now, Princess Indigo, on one of those mountaintops. That's where he is—or at least that's where he was."

Kira looked out the window. Far away to the west, she could see gray stone mountains cutting their jagged peaks against the clear blue sky, and on the highest mountains, stretching far into the distance, Kira could see snowcapped summits standing out like white fingernails on sharp, gray talons.

Kira started to cry. Warm tears filled her eyes, and her shoulders shook up and down with quiet sobs.

Sarah hugged her arms around Kira, squeezing her tight. "You want to see your dad, and that's just what we're going to do. I promise. I'm going to take you there myself. We can leave—"

"Ex-excuse me, Y-Your Majesty," a thin voice called from the doorway.

Kira looked down to see a small, gray rat standing on his hind legs, nervously folding and unfolding his hands as he sniffed the air.

Sarah turned to look at the rat. “Yes, Howard, what is it?”

“It’s just—it seems—what I mean to say is… He’s—he’s here, Your Majesty,” the gray rat finally squeaked.

Sarah dropped her shoulders and sighed. “Of course he is. Then I guess we can leave for the Gryphon Mountains as soon as he’s gone. Is that all right with you, Grand Vizier?”

Kira wiped her eyes and nodded.

“Then we should go to the throne room and receive our guest.” Without waiting for an answer, Sarah turned and walked out of the room. Kira followed her, and Chase and Howard trailed behind them. They crossed the cheese room and went back through the door into the hallway. Then they turned left through another open door, climbed a quick flight of stairs, and turned to the right at the end of the hall.

Now Kira found herself standing in the throne room of the Rat Fort. The room itself was massive—Kira guessed it was big enough to hold her entire house with room to spare. A dozen stained-glass windows decorated the walls on the left and right, filtering cyan-colored sunlight onto the floor below. It made Kira feel like she was stepping inside an aquarium.

Farther in from the walls, six black stone columns stretched from the floor to the ceiling, standing like sentinels on either side of the room. Each one was twice as wide around as the biggest tree Kira had ever seen.

A burgundy carpet led from the far doors to the very center of the floor. It reminded Kira of the red carpet at a Hollywood movie—and in the middle of the room, at the very center, she could see a raised platform and a white marble chair.

It all worked together to make Kira feel very small and timid. Sarah obviously did not feel the same—probably because the beautiful throne at the center of the room was meant for her. She skipped across the floor, hopped between two big cracks in the stone, and then jumped and twirled so that she landed directly in front of the marble chair. Then, with a final jump, she plopped back to sit on the throne.

"Stand next to me, Grand Vizier," Sarah called out, almost singing the words.

Kira did as she was told, taking her place next to the throne.

Sarah looked over at Kira. "This really shouldn't take long. I get these reports on Stony Pointe all the time. I'm not allowed to go there myself, you know." Then she turned to look at Howard. "I think we're ready."

For a second, Kira was confused. Why would Sarah not be allowed to visit Stony Pointe? She was supposed to be the queen, and usually queens could do as they liked. Why would this be different? But then another thought took over in Kira's brain. Howard was halfway to the far doors, and he was about to let someone from Stoney Shore inside the throne room. *Who was it?*

"Sarah, who gives you this report?" Kira asked.

"Oh, a very nice man. He's the mayor of Stony Pointe—Mayor Randolph we call him. I think you'll like him, although I'm not so sure that he likes me very much."

Then Kira was out of time.

Both of the far doors flung open, and Mayor Randolph walked into the room, marching up the burgundy carpet with Howard at his heels.

He stopped in front of the throne and gave a half-bow, leaning forward and tipping his head. "Your Majesty, I've come to deliver my report on Stony Pointe."

Sarah nodded. "Of course, Mayor Randolph. I think we're ready."

Randolph cleared his throat. "Unfortunately, I have some troubling news. I've learned that your villagers have hired a gang of assassins to put an end to your reign. I discovered their leader, a girl with pink hair calling herself Kira, just yesterday—"

Sarah pointed to her right. "You mean *this* Kira? I just made her my Grand Vizier."

Randolph looked to where Sarah was pointing, but his face twisted. "Your Majesty, there's no one there."

Sarah looked for herself, and saw that Randolph was right—there was nothing next to her throne except empty space.

Sarah's mouth dropped open. "Oh my goodness! Maybe she's turned herself invisible—just like my 'H'."

"This isn't a game, Your Majesty!" Randolph growled through his clenched teeth.

"Oh, I know it isn't, Mayor Randolph, because so far this hasn't been any fun. We could try a different game, if you like. Something like hide and seek?" Sarah clapped her hands. "I love hide and seek! Let's do it. Chase!"

A tiny squeak came from inside her tangled hair.

Sarah looked up at her forehead as the white rat walked out of his nest. "There you are, Chase. I want you to go and find Kira, because you're 'it.' Then, when you come back, Mayor Randolph and I will hide, but you need to find me last, because I'm the queen. Do you understand?"

Chase squeaked again, then jumped down from Sarah's head and scurried out of the room.

Sarah looked back at Randolph. "Will you need help finding a hiding place, Mayor Randolph, or will you be okay on your own? I have lots of ideas."

Randolph's face was turning bright red now. "Your Majesty, we don't have time for your make-believe games! You can't play pretend! This girl—this…Kira—she's dangerous!"

Sarah lowered her eyes. "I'm sorry, Mayor Randolph. I won't play pretend anymore. I just thought—"

Randolph reached into his coat pocket. "I have a parchment that needs your signature. This gives me the authority to have Kira arrested on sight and sent back to the Rainbow City to stand trial for her crimes."

Howard dashed to the side of the room and returned with a quill dripping with ink.

Sarah leaned over, took the quill from the rat, and signed her name to the parchment. “Is there anything else, Mayor Randolph?”

Randolph took back the parchment and smiled. “That’s everything I need. I’ll have the girl arrested this afternoon. Her friends, too, if I can find them. Trust me, Your Majesty, you have nothing to fear.”

Then Randolph turned and walked from the room.

*****

“At last, I’ve found you!” Chase squeaked, standing on the rail of the balcony overlooking the throne room.

Kira jumped inside her own skin, but before the rat could squeak again, she raised her finger to her lips, urging him to stay quiet.

The rat turned his head to one side. “Excuse me, Princess, but perhaps you can explain why you’re way up here?”

Kira looked down. The floor of the throne room was far below her. In fact, if she reached up with her hand, Kira thought she could probably touch the ceiling. She leaned her head back against the black stone column behind her. From this angle, she could just see the corner of the white throne and one of Sarah's feet tapping against the floor.

From either side of Kira's shoulders, huge, purple butterfly wings wafted back and forth, holding her afloat in midair. It was the only thing she could think to do.

When Sarah told her that Mayor Randolph was about to step into the throne room, Kira knew she had to hide. She didn't trust that man—and now, having overheard his conversation with Sarah, she knew it was for good reason.

Kira looked back at Chase. "That man down there is a liar."

"Of course he is, Princess," Chase squeaked. "In fact, all the rats here think so too, but I'm afraid Her Majesty trusts him. So you see, there's really nothing we can do."

"Of course there is. We just need to find someone from Stony Pointe to tell Sarah the truth—someone who has experience with Mayor Randolph and his lies. And I know just the person. I want you to go to the village and find a girl named Chloe. She has dark hair and she wears it in braided pigtails. Find her and bring her back to the Rat Fort."

The tiny rat bowed his head. "If you think this will help Her Majesty, then I will do everything I can."

Without another word, Chase scampered away.

Chapter 13: Reunited

“There you are!” Sarah shouted, pointing her finger at Kira.

Kira floated to the ground, her purple butterfly wings fluttering in the air like tissue paper caught in a summer breeze. Then, as her foot touched the floor, the wings evaporated in a cloud of purple mist.

Sarah clapped her hands. “I’m so glad that you’re real. Mayor Randolph said he thought you were just pretend, but then you were invisible, so I thought maybe he was right. But now you’re visible again, and that definitely means you’re real. Can you believe there's another girl named Kira who also has pink hair? That's amazing, right?"

Kira smiled. "Sarah, I think Mayor Randolph was talking about me."

Sarah shook her head. "Absolutely not! He thinks you're made up, remember? He's talking about this other Kira. But now he's gone, so we can do what we want. Tell me, Grand Vizier, should we set out for the Gryphon Mountains at once, or should we free your friends from the dungeon first?"

Kira stifled a laugh. "I think my friends would like to come with us, actually."

"Then let's go get them." Sarah walked from the throne room and turned right down a long, carpeted hallway. Kira thought the passage looked familiar, but she had seen so many halls and doors in the Rat Fort that it was impossible to tell for sure.

Kira looked at Sarah. The girl was walking next to her, sashaying left and right down the corridor, humming a soft melody to herself without a care in the world.

"Sarah," Kira interrupted the girl's humming, "you mentioned something before ,and I can't figure it out. Why aren't you *allowed* to go to Stony Pointe?"

Then Sarah's smile fell away. "I can't go there because it's too dangerous. Mayor Randolph says the villagers don't like me at all. He says they would hurt me if they could. That's why he hired Mr. Pike and his steam bandits. They're supposed to keep the villagers away from the Rat Fort, so I can be safe."

Kira's face twisted. "Is that why you make them collect extra money from the villagers? So you can pay them to protect you?"

"Extra money?" Sarah laughed. "I don't collect *any* money from the villagers! I make cheese, remember? I thought I told you."

Then Kira understood what was happening. Mayor Randolph and Pike were working together. Pike ordered his men to collect taxes from the villagers, and Mayor Randolph told Sarah she needed to pay the steam bandits for protection, but really they kept all the money for themselves.

Kira stamped her foot on the carpet. "The villagers of Stony Pointe are afraid of you, Sarah!"

Sarah turned her head to one side. "That's not what Mayor Randolph says. He says *I* should be afraid of *them*."

"Well, Mayor Randolph is lying!"

Sarah laughed again. "I don't think so, Kira. I mean, I gave Mayor Randolph the same test I gave you. That means I can trust him, you know."

"But we're saying opposite things!" Kira shouted. "How can you believe us both?"

Sarah shrugged her shoulders. "It's a paradox, I guess, but who can understand those things?"

Then she started again down the hallway. Kira had no choice but to follow. At the next door, Sarah pushed it open and stepped inside.

Now they were back in the dungeon, at the top of the steps. On the floor below, Kira could see her three friends, still chained to the wall. They all looked up, and when they saw Kira standing at the top of the stairs, wide grins broke over all their faces.

"Princess, you're safe!" Snugg shouted.

Kira ran down the stairs and scooped the tiny bear up in a hug. “I am. In fact, I was never in danger. None of us were.”

Fred climbed to his feet. “And I see you’ve made a new friend.” The zombie looked to the top of the stairs. “What’s your name, miss?”

Sarah skipped down the stairs, jumping over the last two, and landing in a deep curtsey in front of the prisoners. “I’m Sarah, with an ‘H,’ but that’s invisible right now. I’m also the Rat Queen, or the Queen of the Rats—I’m still not sure which one I prefer.”

“The Rat Queen? Then you’re crazy!” Ben blurted out the words before he could stop himself. Then, everyone else fell quiet.

Sarah stepped closer to Ben, focusing her eyes directly on the end of his nose. “That’s not a very nice thing to say.”

“And it’s not true,” Kira added, stepping next to Sarah.

Ben looked down at the floor and took a step back, but that was as far as he could go. Now his back was against the wall. "I'm sorry. It's just that—I mean, everyone says that you're completely crazy. Those are the rumors."

Sarah stepped back, and now she was smiling again. "My grandfather says that rumors and reputation are just illusions. They're the lies people see when they don't care about learning the truth."

"Then tell us the truth," Ben said, staring back at Sarah. "Are you really crazy?"

Sarah laughed. "That's a silly question to ask. Most crazy people don't know that they're crazy, or at least they won't admit it, so more often than not the answer will be 'no,' but that's not always the truth. I do talk to Dr. Manuel once a week, and he says I'm *not* crazy. He says we all just need help sometimes."

As Sarah talked, Kira's own memory drifted back to third grade. That's when her teacher sent her to talk to the school counselor, Mrs. Kinney. It was only October, but Kira had been crying every day in school—usually because of something Sophia had done. It made Kira feel better to talk about what she was feeling. Of course, Sophia found out where Kira was going, and then she started calling her "Crazy Kira" for the entire month of November. It made Kira so mad, and even now, thinking about the memory, she could feel herself getting angry again.

"Sarah's not crazy," Kira said, locking her jaw. "She's kind, and smart, and funny. And she's right, everyone needs help sometimes. *Everyone*."

"Like all of you need my help right now, because you're chained to the wall." Sara raised her voice, shouting into the dungeon. "Carlos! Patrick! Bradley! Would you please unlock our guests?"

Three brown rats raced out of the shadows of the dungeon. They climbed up the walls, jumped across to the chains hanging around the three companions, and in less than a second, the shackles fell away, clanking to the floor.

"I suppose you're all hungry," Sarah said, but before Ben, Fred, or Snugg could answer, she turned to her trio of rats. "Bradley, I want you to go and set the grand dining room for a snack. Carlos and Patrick can help you. We can have tea and cheese, and if we don't have any tea, we can have cheese and cheese. Cheese for a snack and cheese for a drink. It's actually quite good, you know, when it's all warm and melty. How does that sound?"

Snugg and Ben stared straight ahead without answering—the idea of both eating cheese and *drinking* cheese still turning in their brains—but Fred didn't hesitate.

The zombie bowed at the waist. "Cheese and cheese sounds lovely, Your Majesty. Thank you for the offer."

Sarah jumped and clapped her hands. "Now we just need to find Chase. Where is that rat? Chase!"

Kira felt a wave of panic crash over her. She was the one who sent Chase to find Chloe, but now that the rat was gone, and she thought maybe she had made a mistake. *Would Sarah be angry that Kira sent her most trusted rat on a secret mission?*

Kira cleared her throat. "Your Majesty, I sent Chase on an errand… for me. I hope you don't mind."

"Actually, Y-Your Majesty…" The tiny voice came from the top of the stairs. Everyone looked up, and they could see Howard standing just inside the door. The small gray rat was folding and unfolding his hands. "I-I wanted to tell you that Chase—He's—he's returned to the castle, and he's… Well, he's brought a friend."

"That's perfect." Sarah clapped her hands again. "You can send them both to the dining room. We'll have our cheese and cheese together. This way, friends."

Sarah marched back up the dungeon stairs. Kira, Snugg, Ben, and Fred all followed. This time they turned down a hallway and arrived at a set of tall double doors.

Sarah pulled them both open and walked through into what must have been the grand dining room. Kira could see a long wooden table with at least twenty high-backed chairs lined up around it. The table was covered with a white table cloth and set with dishes and shining silver forks and knives. It all looked very elegant, like they were about to sit down to a holiday feast rather than a mid-afternoon snack.

Chase was already waiting in the room, standing on his hind legs on top of the table. And seated at the far end of the room, Kira could see his guest. It was Chloe.

As soon as Kira stepped into the room, Chloe bolted out of her seat, running to meet her. She threw her arms around Kira's neck, hugging her tight.

Then all of Chloe's words spilled out at once, running together. "You're here! And you're safe. And you're not captured. But where's your dad? And why are you still here, anyway? And where's that ol' Rat Queen?"

Sarah waved. "Hello, friend."

Chloe pointed at her. "And who are you supposed to be?"

"I'm Sarah, and I'm the Rat Queen—not sure about the 'old' part, though. I certainly don't feel old."

Then Chloe grabbed Kira by the arm. "Get behind me, Princess."

But Kira held her ground. “Chloe, it’s not what you think. Sarah’s not dangerous. Not at all. She’s my cousin.”

“But more like sisters, really.” Sarah looped her arm around Kira’s shoulders.

Kira shook her head and tried to focus. “It’s good to see you again, Chloe.”

“It is, but to tell you the truth, I ain’t really sure why I’m here. I went into town looking for you when y’all didn’t show up at the farm this mornin’. Then I met this here rat.” Chloe pointed down at Chase, still standing at the end of the table. “He drew your picture in the dirt, complete with a pink rose petal for your hair, so I figured you must be in some sort of trouble or something.”

Sarah looked at the rat. “This is Chase, my seneschal. Kira sent him to bring you here, I guess.”

Chase lowered his head. “I’m sorry, Your Majesty, but it’s much more than that. You see, I’ve brought this girl Chloe so that you can learn the truth about that vile man, Mayor Randolph. I found her listening to his lies at the tavern window this morning. She can tell you the rest for herself."

Sarah turned to Chloe. "Chase says you were listening to Mayor Randolph at the tavern. What was he saying?"

"More of his lies." Chloe folded her arms across her chest. "I heard him going on and on through the window. He said Kira was a spy for the Rat Queen. Then he said Kira told you to triple our taxes. He said we should take that money and bribe the steam bandits instead. He said they would kidnap Kira and carry her away to someplace else."

Sarah stepped back from the table. "But that's not true! Mayor Randolph is lying. Kira's not my spy! And I don't collect *any* taxes from Stony Pointe. I just make cheese."

"Don't collect taxes!?" Chloe yelled in disbelief. "You've been taking our money twice a week for a while now. We ain't got no money left to pay your taxes."

Kira put her hand on Chloe's shoulder. "But it's not Sarah taking your money. She's telling the truth.

She only wants to make cheese. It's Pike and Randolph—they're in this together, stealing from everyone."

Sarah pulled out one of the chairs and sat down. She leaned forward, putting both her elbows on the table and cradling her head in her hands, staring down at the floor. Then, for a long while, no one spoke.

Finally, Sarah looked up. "So what do we do now, Grand Vizier?"

Kira already knew the answer—she knew what had to be done as soon as Chloe told them the lies Mayor Randolph was spreading in the tavern—but that didn't make it any easier to say out loud.

Kira took a deep breath. Then she forced herself to answer, "We go to Stony Pointe—together—and we tell them the truth."

Chapter 14: What Friends Do

"I can't go to Stony Pointe. I already told you: it's dangerous." Sarah stood up from her chair and walked to the far side of the table.

Kira followed after her. "Mayor Randolph told you that. Now you know he's a liar. You're the Rat Queen, Sarah. You can do whatever you want."

Sarah wheeled around to face Kira, pointing her finger across the table at Chloe. "Your *friend* over there wanted to tackle me as soon as I told her I was the Rat Queen."

Kira laughed. "That's ridiculous Chloe would never—"

"Of course I did," Chloe interrupted, staring across the table at the two girls.

"What?" Kira couldn't believe what she was hearing. She turned to look at Chloe.

Chloe shrugged. "She's the Rat Queen, so I thought she deserved it. I actually thought about hittin' her over the head with one of these plates."

"You're not helping." Kira said.

Chloe laughed to herself. "Well, I ain't trying to be difficult neither, but Sarah's right. The people in Stony Pointe don't like her."

Kira shook her head. "That's all the more reason why they need to hear the truth."

"But it won't be that simple, Princess," Snugg growled from the end of the table, and everyone turned to look.

"What do you mean, Snugg?" Kira asked.

The tiny bear rubbed his paw back and forth over his chin. "Randolph is a liar and a cheat—we can deal with him by telling the truth—but Pike is something else altogether. He won't just walk away from this village or their money. He's going to want blood."

Fred smiled. "And when have you ever shied away from a fight, old friend?"

"Not me." Snugg shook his head. "It's not my decision, but If we do this, the princess needs to understand what she's asking. She needs to know where this ends."

Kira looked down at the table. Snugg was right—it would take more than the truth to rip Stony Pointe free from Pike and his steam bandits. Could she ask anyone to take that chance, knowing the fight that would follow? *What would her dad say?*

Kira remembered sitting in the car with her father… *"If anyone ever tries to hurt you, Kira—you or any of your friends—you fight them. You fight and you win."*

Kira looked up at the others. "I can't control what Pike will do. I can't control Randolph, or the steam bandits, or the villagers. I can only do what I think is right, and if I have to defend myself—or my friends—I'm ready."

Chloe shook her head. "That's all well and good for you and me, Kira, but these villagers ain't fighters. I know 'em, and I'm tellin' you, they ain't got it in 'em."

Kira looked across the table. "Then we'll have to fight *for* them. If we can gather the villagers in the center of town—if we can all stand there together—then we'll have a chance."

"Or we can just stay here, safe in the Rat Fort." Sarah clapped her hands. "Wouldn't that be more fun? I have plenty of cheese and lots of board games, and we can just wait for the steam bandits to leave on their own. What do you think?"

"I think you're scared." Ben answered before anyone else could speak, and for a second, his words hung in the air, expanding into the silence.

Sarah forced a smile. "Maybe I am scared. So what?"

"I'm scared, too," Ben said, looking around the table at the others. "I think we're all scared, but it doesn't matter. Kira's right—the villagers deserve the truth."

Sarah laughed. "And I guess you're some kind of expert on what kings and queens are supposed to do for their people?"

Ben shook his head. "I don't know anything about that. I don't know what kings or queens or princesses for that matter are *supposed* to do, but it's what a friend would do."

"Kira and I *are* friends," Sarah said.

"Then help me, Sarah. Please." Kira reached for Sarah's hand. "You're the Rat Queen; we won't stand a chance without you."

Sarah smiled. "And we're also friends. Best sister-cousin-friends forever, right?"

Kira laughed. Sarah had called them that before, but the first time she said it—best sister-cousin-friends—it didn't mean anything. Kira hardly knew the girl. But now… now things were different. Sarah was kind, and weird, and kind of weirdly perfect. She was Kira's friend—and more than a friend, she was family. That made Sarah the closest thing to a sister she ever had. Kira laughed again, and now she could feel tears starting in her eyes.

"Of course we are!" Kira threw both her arms around Sarah. "Best sister-cousin-friends forever!"

Sarah started laughing too. Then she wiggled free from Kira's hug and turned back to face the others. "So I guess we're going to Stony Pointe."

*****

The walk to the village was a short one. Kira followed Sarah through the castle twisting left and right through what felt like an endless maze of hallways that all looked the same. Chloe, Ben, Fred, and Snugg all walked single-file behind her. None of them spoke. Finally, Sarah led them through a pair of heavy wooden doors. They were outside now. Kira could see the bright sky overhead. It was almost noon.

The companions crossed an open courtyard, and then they stepped through another pair of studded, wooden doors. Now they were outside of the Rat Fort, standing on the black stone bridge leading to the mainland. In the distance, Kira could see the pitched roofs of the village rising in front of her, and from behind, she could hear the grating metal of the portcullis falling into place. It gave Kira a sick feeling, like spiders were crawling down her back.

Once they crossed the bridge, Chloe took the lead. She marched up the trail ahead of them, and Kira and her friends followed. It was an easy trip. The dirt path to the village was wide and the slope was gentle, but the closer they got to Stony Pointe, the slower they seemed to walk.

Kira knew the reason; she could feel it in her own stomach as it got tighter and twistier with every step. She was nervous—more than nervous, she was afraid. But even walking slowly, there was no time left to change her mind. They were already standing in the center of the village.

"Doesn't look too friendly, does it?" Sarah leaned over and whispered to Kira.

Kira looked around. Sarah was right. Up and down, in every direction, the village of Stony Pointe seemed abandoned—not a single person anywhere in sight.

Kira turned to Chloe. "Where is everyone?"

Chloe shrugged. "I'm not sure. Let me try something." She stepped to the corner where a large, metal ring swayed in the breeze between two wooden posts. Kira had seen something like it before in front of the firehouse near her home. Her father told her it was an old-fashioned fire alarm.

Chloe picked up the metal rod hanging next to the ring, and she started swinging it back and forth, battering the inside of the ring, and a loud clanging alarm rose over the town.

All at once, doors kicked open and men came running out of the buildings followed by women and children, all of them ready to help with whatever emergency caused the alarm, but when they saw who was behind the ringing—and when they saw Kira and her friends standing nearby—the running stopped. Now the people inched forward, none of them daring to step too close.

"What's the meaning of all this?" Mayor Randolph's voice roared from the back of the crowd.

Then the people shuffled out of the way, and Randolph stepped to the center of the crowd.

At first, Kira thought he looked confused. His eyes looked over them all trying to understand what would bring them here, and why they would be standing together. Then he focused on Kira, and she could see his face change—Randolph understood now. His eyes narrowed and his skin turned dark red.

"What do you think you're doing here," Randolph roared again.

But Kira didn't answer—at least not to him. Instead, she looked past Randolph and raised her voice to the crowd. "My name is Princess Kira the First, Defender of the Kingdoms, Lady of the Unicorn Spire, Queen of the Zombies, Grand Vizier of the Rat Fort, and Heiress to the Rainbow Throne. I am not a spy. I am not an assassin. Those are lies, and I'm here to tell you the truth."

Kira turned to Sarah. "You don't know my friend, but this is Sarah. She's the daughter of Princess Indigo. She's the ruler of the Garden, and she's the Queen of the Rats."

As soon as Kira spoke, hushed whispers swept over the crowd, everyone asking a hundred questions.

Sarah was confused, too—she leaned closer to Kira. “What am I supposed to do now?”

Kira smiled. Then she put her hand on Sarah’s shoulder. “This is the easy part. You tell them the truth.”

Sarah stepped forward, shouting over the crowd. “Hello.”

The crowd fell silent.

Sarah cleared her throat. “Well… uh… Kira was telling you the truth. My name really is Sarah. I suppose you can spell that however you like, but there is an ‘H’ in there… somewhere. I’m also the Rat Queen, or the Queen of the Rats, if you prefer. Mayor Randolph told me Stony Pointe was dangerous. I guess you don’t like me too much because of all the taxes. The thing is, I never asked for your money—I don’t want your money. Believe it or not, I’ve actually been paying the steam bandits to keep me safe from you.”

"You're a liar!" Mayor Randolph's voice roared again over the crowd. "This girl isn't even the Rat Queen. I've never seen her before in my life!"

Just then, Chase jumped out of Sarah's hair, landing in front of her on the ground and making an angry squeak.

Mayor Randolph recoiled back from the rodent, raising one foot off the ground, twisting his body away, and screaming, "Eeeeaahh!"

Everyone in the crowd laughed.

Chloe stepped forward. "Are you sure she's the one lyin', Mayor Randolph? I've been inside the Rat Fort. I didn't see any of our money layin' around, and I sure didn't see any of my grandpa's furniture those steam bandits took when we ran out of money. What'll we see in your house?"

"No one's going anywhere near my house," Randolph barked.

Then more whispers swept over the crowd, and they sounded angry.

Randolph's face changed again. It wasn't red anymore—now it was closer to white—and his eyes darted left and right as he tried to back pedal his way through the crowd. Only this time the villagers didn't move. They held their ground, trapping him at the center of their congregation.

Randolph turned around and shouted at the villagers. "These girls are crazy!"

Sarah shook her head. "That's not a nice word, Mayor Randolph."

"You all know me!" he shouted again.

"And y'all know me," Chloe answered, just as loud as the mayor. "Y'all know I don't lie."

"It's a simple question," Kira raised her voice now, and everyone in the crowd fell silent again. "Are you going to believe Mayor Randolph, or are you going to believe all of us?"

Suddenly, a strong hand from the crowd grabbed Randolph by the back of his collar.

"What are you— What are you doing? Unhand me, sir! I demand you let me go!" Randolph tried to twist around to see who had him.

An old face with a bushy orange mustache peeked over his shoulder—it was Sheriff Quincy. "What should we do with him, Yer Majesty?"

For a second, no one answered.

Kira leaned over to Sarah. "I think he's asking you."

"Oh… uh… I mean, of course." Sarah stepped forward, raising her hand as if she were about to deliver some grand declaration, but then, just as quickly as she stepped forward, her hand fell to her side and she stepped back. "What *should* we do with him, Grand Vizier?"

Kira smiled. "I'd put him in the jail, at least for now."

Sarah stepped forward again, lifting her hand and raising her voice so everyone in the crowd could hear. "You can take Mayor Randolph to the jail."

The crowd erupted in cheers and applause, jumping and clapping and dancing—and all Sarah could do was laugh.

Chapter 15: Battle for Stony Pointe

"Everyone listen! Please!" Kira tried to shout over the crowd, raising both of her arms to quiet them down. Just as the noise fell, Sheriff Quincy turned Mayor Randolph away and started toward the jail. Then another cheer rose from the crowd, punctuated by loud laughter from all the children.

"The princess is talking," Snugg roared, and it was a frightening sound, louder than all the cheering from the crowd. Then the people of Stony Pointe fell silent, their eyes turning to Kira.

"Mayor Randolph was only part of the problem," Kira said. "When the steam bandits find out what we've done—that we've locked Mayor Randolph in the jail—they won't be happy. We need to prepare—"

"Oh, I think you have worse problems than that, Kira," a thin voice called out from behind the crowd. Then the villagers parted to the sides of the street, and Kira could see who stood behind them.

It was Pike. The tall man stood in the middle of the road wearing his brown coat and his rumpled top hat, and behind him, Kira could see a gang of men, most of their swords already drawn.

Pike smiled, his pale crooked teeth filling the bottom half of his face. "Seems like we're early."

Kira took a deep breath, steadying her voice. "I understand that you're angry, Pike. Let's go to the inn and talk about it. I'm sure we can reach some compromise."

Pike chuckled, "Oh, I don't feel much like talking right now, Kira, so let's try this instead: You give us Randolph right now, and we'll only burn a couple of your houses to the ground. How's that for a compromise?"

"I won't let you do that!" Sarah shouted, stepping forward as if she might charge headlong at Pike herself, but Kira grabbed her arm and pulled her back.

"We don't want to fight you, Pike," Kira shouted.

Pike laughed again. "Well, that's funny, Kira, because I have thirty men with me, and they *all* want to fight you."

A jolt of panic started in Kira's toes and raced up to her stomach, but she refused to let it show on her face. Instead, she took a deep breath and shouted back, "You only have thirty men. We have over a hundred!"

Pike grinned. "Maybe you do, Kira. Maybe that's exactly how many villagers you have, but my men all have swords."

"We have hammers," a voice shouted from the crowd.

"And we have rakes," another voice added. "Or… some of us have rakes!"

Pike's smile stretched across his face. "Like I said, Kira, my men all have swords, and we've been spoiling for a fight. Last chance."

The high-pitched whine of the steam-swords rose into the air, as the serrated blades started cutting back and forth.

Kira drew her rapier from its sheath and shouted to the villagers. "We need to stand together. Form a circle. Stand shoulder to shoulder. Keep the children in the center."

"Brog," Pike leaned over to speak to the bald man at this side. "I want you to go and break that crowd apart."

Brog touched his hand to his chest. "Me, sir? Are you sure?"

"Yes, I'm sure!" Pike grabbed Brog's arm and jerked him toward the crowd of villagers.

The bald man stumbled forward a couple of steps, but then he caught himself. He turned back to Pike, shaking his head. "I want to, sir—really. It's just… I mean, they have that bear."

"You think I'm worried about some teddy bear?!?" Pike shouted in Brog's face, but before Brog could answer—before the bald man could move—Snugg stepped out from the crowd.

Brog looked over his shoulder. All the color drained from the bald man's face and his arms and legs started to shake.

"What are you doing?" Kira called after Snugg.

"Finishing what I started," Snugg growled

Then the bear's claws popped free of his stuffed paws, and with a wordless roar, Snugg charged at the line of steam bandits.

"Eeeeeeeehhhh!" Brog's voice broke into a high-pitched shriek. Then he sprinted to his left, running away from the village as fast as he could, with Snugg chasing after him.

Then Pike was tired of waiting. He drew his sword and shouted, "Everyone attack!"

The steam bandits ran forward, shouting angry, wordless screams. The villagers answered with a rolling cry of their own. Then swinging steam-swords met hammers, and rakes, and buckets, and spoons, and anything else the villagers had grabbed to defend themselves.

Kira screamed over the sounds of fighting. “Stay together! Don’t let them draw you out! Protect our center!”

From her right, a steam-sword swung at her head. Kira raised her rapier to block it. For a second, she stood face to face with the man, his red-whiskered chin only inches from her own. Then, out of nowhere, a green fist connected with the side of the steam bandit’s face, and the man reeled back from the crowd.

Kira looked to her left and saw Fred shaking out his hand. “You keep giving orders, Princess. I’ll protect you from these ruffians.”

Then Kira turned and screamed. “Keep fighting everyone! Stay in the circle! Draw them in closer!”

“It won’t matter, girl,” someone shouted over the chaos.

Kira spun in the direction of the voice. It was that spiky-haired Jagan, staring at her from outside the crowd of villagers.

"You think you're going to save them? This whole village is going to burn," Jagan shouted.

Kira clenched her teeth and felt her blood rise into her face. She wanted to charge straight at Jagan. She wanted to knock him to the ground and drag him into the jail next to Randolph. But that's what Jagan wanted too. He was baiting her, trying to get Kira to make a mistake. She wouldn't let it work.

"I'll take care of him," Ben called out.

"Wait," Kira shouted, but it was already too late. Ben leapt forward from the crowd, swinging his sword through the air.

Jagan easily turned the blow aside. "The cook? Are you trying to fight me? I was hoping to see you again, boy."

"Well here I am." Ben swung his sword again, but Jagan was too fast. Ben tried again, and again, and again—left, right, and then he stabbed straight at Jagan's chest—but each time the steam bandit parried, or dodged, or blocked. It was useless.

Jagan laughed. "Give up, cook! You're no good at this. You should have stayed in the kitchen chopping vegetables."

Ben nodded. "Maybe you're right, but I only need to distract you."

Jagan's face twisted. "Distract me from what?"

CLANG!

Jagan's eyes crossed, and he pitched forward, landing flat on his face. Behind him, Chloe swung her frying pan back over her shoulder.

She pointed down at Jagan. "That's twice, you varmint!"

Ben smiled. "Let's hope there's not a third." Then he grabbed Chloe's other hand and dragged her back to the crowd of villagers.

"Close the circle!" Kira screamed again. "Draw them in closer! Even closer!"

Kira looked to her right. Sarah stood next to her.

"Are you ready?" Kira asked.

Sarah nodded. Then she cupped her hands over her mouth and screamed, "Rats! Make Ready!"

Then a new sound filled the air, louder than the ringing metal of battle or the whine of the steam-swords. It was squeaking.

Then the sounds of the fighting died away. No one was swinging swords or frying pans anymore. They all just stood there—steam bandits and villagers alike—all of them staring out at the buildings around the center of town.

The squeaking grew even louder, and then, on the roof of a building, a single rat rose up on its hind legs. He was thin and gray, and Kira recognized him at once. It was Howard… but now he wasn't standing alone.

More rats rose up—James and Cole and Shane. They stood behind Howard on the rooftop, looking down on the crowd of people at the center of the village. Then even more rats appeared. They lined the rooftops and squeezed between cracks in the walls of the buildings, and filled the empty roads—tens of thousands of rats—all of them perched on their hind legs, their thin, pink noses sniffing at the air, waiting.

Sarah shouted again. "Rats! Attack!"

The rats surged forward. They jumped from the roofs and sprinted across the roads like a tidal wave of gray fur racing to meet the shore.

"Stay together!" Kira shouted, and the villagers held their ground.

At first, some of the steam bandits tried to kick at the rats, but it was useless. For every rat they kicked, five more would take its place. Then the steam bandits turned to run. The rats swarmed over them, clinging to their pants and backs and shoulders. Some of the steam bandits fell, and the rats covered over them like heavy snow in winter. The rest of them kept on their feet, but the army of rats still chased after them, biting at their heels, and the gray fur looked like fog curling over the road.

For a long moment after, the villagers stood frozen in their circle, everyone watching as the steam bandits ran away from the village. No one dared to speak.

Kira was still watching when she felt someone tugging at her fingers. She looked down and saw a small girl, her face smudged with dirt across her nose, and her blonde hair pulled back in a ponytail. She couldn't have been older than three.

"Yes?" Kira said. In the stillness of the moment, her voice sounded very loud.

The little girl stepped back and rubbed her eyes. "Princess, is it over?"

Kira knelt down beside the girl. "I'm not sure. I think you should ask your queen."

The little girl turned to Sarah. "Is it over?"

Sarah nodded. "It is. You're safe now. I think we all are."

Then the crowd of villagers cheered again—clapping their hands and raising their arms—and Sarah was laughing again too, just like before, but this time it proved contagious. Soon everyone in the village was laughing and shaking hands and hugging one another—and Kira was at the center of it all.

Chapter 16: The Road From the Village

As the laughter and cheers faded in the air, a group of villagers brought forward three men held as prisoners—three steam bandits who failed to escape the army of rats. Their hands were already tied together by rope, and each one stared silently down at the dirt. Two of the men Kira had never seen before, but the third prisoner she recognized. It was Jagan.

Samuel, the innkeeper, stepped in front of the prisoners and dropped to his knee. "Your Majesty, what should we do with these men?"

Sarah tapped her foot. "What *should* we do? Grand Vizier, what do you think?"

A growling voice answered before Kira could speak. "We should put them in jail with Randolph, where they belong."

Kira looked past the prisoners in the direction of the voice, and she could see Snugg walking up the road. The tiny bear smiled and winked his marble eye.

"Snugg, you're all right!" Kira shouted.

Then Snugg ran forward, past the prisoners, and jumped into Kira's outstretched arms, hugging her tight around her neck.

"Of course I'm all right. So are you, I see."

Kira lowered the bear back to the ground. "My plan worked, Snugg. As soon as Sarah called for her rats, the steam bandits all turned and ran."

The bear laughed. "I know it, Princess. I saw it. I passed them all running away on the road. I'm so proud of you. I know your parents would be proud as well."

Then Kira felt proud of herself. She smiled at the bear. "And what about Pike? Did you see him running away, too?"

"Of course I did. He was the first one I saw running away, leading the others out of town—the coward."

Kira frowned. Of all the steam bandits, Pike was the one she hoped to capture the most. Even so, if he was running away like Snugg said, it was just as good. There was no way he would risk coming back to Stony Pointe now.

"And what about Brog?" Kira asked.

Snugg rubbed his chin and smiled. "I let Brog go. Trust me, Princess, he learned his lesson. His days of being a steam bandit are over."

"Me too! I've learned my lesson." Jagan tried to step forward, but Samuel rose to his feet and grabbed him by the shoulder.

Kira looked at Jagan. He certainly *looked* different—like he was finally scared of what might happen to him. Maybe being covered over by a thousand rats had that effect on a person.

Kira raised her voice. "Your Majesty, I suggest we do what Snugg said, put these men in jail next to Mayor Randolph, as long as there's room."

Sheriff Quincy stood at the side of the crowd and nodded. "Yep, we got plenty of room for these 'uns. You jus' say the word, Yer Majesty."

Sarah stood up straight in front of the prisoners, and she forced herself to stop smiling. "Very well. I want you to put these men in jail for… For at least two weeks."

"Oh, thank you. Thank you, Your Majesty. Thank you," Jagan said, and the prisoners standing next to him echoed the words over and over. Then Sarah waved her hand, and Samuel led them away.

She turned back to Kira. "Now, I think it's time for more important decisions."

Kira's nose wrinkled. "Decisions about what?"

Sarah reached down and took hold of both of Kira's hands. "I told you that we would go and find your father. Now that Stony Pointe is safe, it's time for us to leave. I already know who I'm going to leave in charge of the Rat Fort. Chase!"

As she called out his name, Chase scurried forward from the crowd of people, stopping in front of Kira and Sarah and rising up on his hind legs.

"Chase, I want you to take care of the Rat Fort while I'm gone," Sarah said.

Then Chase bowed deeply at the waist. "My deepest apologies, Your Majesty, but I cannot be left in command of your fortress. Honor demands that I never leave your side, and so instead I beg you, please, Your Majesty, don't leave me behind."

Sarah shook her head. "But if I take you with me, who's going to watch the Rat Fort, silly?"

Chase bowed his head again. "I don't want to overstep my bounds, Your Majesty, but… it seems Howard would be an excellent choice, Your Majesty. I think he's proved himself more than capable."

"All right." Then Sara raised her voice again, "Howard!"

In less than a second, the thin, gray rat scampered forward to stand next to Chase. "Yes, Y-Your Majesty?"

Sarah smiled. "Chase thinks you should watch the Rat Fort while we're gone, and I think so, too."

The little rat's face lit up. "Oh—oh, yes, Your Majesty. I-I would be honored."

"Then it's settled. Now I only need to find someone to watch the village. Any ideas for a new mayor, Grand Vizier?"

Kira smiled—the question was easy. She leaned forward and whispered in Sarah's ear. Then Sarah laughed, jumped in the air, and clapped her hands. "Of course! It's too perfect."

She turned to face the villagers. "Men and women of Stony Pointe, I hereby proclaim that our newest friend Chloe shall be the mayor of your village. Long live Mayor Chloe!"

The crowd echoed the cheer. "Long live Mayor Chloe!"

But Chloe stepped forward, shaking her head. "Wait a minute, Your Majesty. I think you made some mistake. I don't know nothing about being a mayor of anything."

Sarah shrugged. "Neither do I… because I'm not a mayor—I'm a queen, you see—but I can't imagine it's too difficult. Try your best to keep everyone safe. Guard the people against injustice, and help wherever you can. I know you can do at least that much, because you already have. Will you accept?"

Chloe looked down at the dirt, kicking at a rock. "I guess it don't sound like too much trouble, if you really think I can do it."

Kira put her hand on the girl's shoulder. "You're going to be a great mayor, Chloe."

"Perfect." Sarah clapped her hands. Then she turned back to the crowd. "Now that we're all settled, it really is time for Princess Kira and myself to set off on our journey—"

"Just one more second there, Yer Majesty," Sheriff Quincy interrupted.

Sarah turned back in the direction of the voice. "Yes? What is it, mustachioed-man?"

Quincy poked his finger against the brim on his hat, forcing it up over his bushy orange eyebrows. "Not quite sure who that is you're talking about, Yer

Majesty, but if yer talkin' about me, my name's Quincy, and I'm the sheriff of this here town."

Sarah pulled out the hem of her dress and curtseyed. "Pleased to meet you, Sheriff."

Quincy shook his head. "Pleasure's all mine, Miss, but I got more to say than just introductions. Ya'll saved us today, and it seems the reason we needed savin' at all is because I didn't do my job. Your mother made me sheriff of Stony Pointe, and I was charged with keeping these people safe. Instead, I let Mayor Randolph and those steam bandits right into the sheep's pen. In my book, that means I owe ya. So if yer set on goin' off on some adventure today, seems the least I can do is get ya there safe—that is, if you'll have me."

Sarah looked over her shoulder at Kira.

Kira nodded. "Of course we'll have you, Sheriff, gladly."

The crowd of villagers cheered again as they parted to either side of the road. Then, with a final wave, Sarah started out of the village. Kira followed, and Fred, Ben, and Snugg all fell into line behind her. Sheriff Quincy brought up the rear.

Sarah set a quick pace out of the village, and within five minutes, they passed the last of the houses. Then nothing lay before them but the road, the forest, and rising high above the trees in the distance, the gray stone peaks of the Gryphon Mountains.

Chapter 17: Up the Mountain

They walked for the rest of the day, and finally stopped at the base of the mountain. In fact, it seemed like Sarah would have been happy to keep walking through the night. She insisted she knew the way—that she could get there with her eyes closed—and she would be happy to prove it by leading them up the mountain in the dark. It was only after Fred convinced her that the others would get lost that Sarah finally gave up.

They made camp with a small fire at the center, and their sleeping blankets laid out like spokes in a wheel. Kira thought it was nice to be sleeping outside again. She closed her eyes and fell asleep before she even realized.

*****

The next morning, Kira woke up to the warm smell of food and the crackling sounds of grease in the bottom of a skillet.

She sat straight up and took a deep sniff through her nose. “That smells delicious. What is it?”

Ben lifted up the frying pan, tilting it to one side so Kira could see for herself, but as soon as he did, Kira scrunched up her nose and stuck out her tongue.

“What’s wrong?” Ben asked. “It’s only fish. Snugg and I found a stream this morning. I thought you said it smelled good.”

Kira had only tried fish once in her life. Her mother made her eat salmon for dinner one night. Kira took the smallest bite possible, immediately declared she didn’t like it, and she hadn’t tried it since. Only now she was very hungry, and it did smell *very* good.

“All right,” she said, “I’ll try some, but just a little.”

After another minute of cooking, Ben declared that breakfast was ready. Kira picked up her piece of fish and took a bite. It was good. She took another bite—and another—and before she knew it, her breakfast was gone. Then she was disappointed there was none left over for seconds.

After breakfast was over, camp was packed, and the companions began their climb up the mountain. Kira had been on hikes before with both of her parents, but she had never tried anything like this. The Gryphon Mountains were rocky and steep, and Kira knew that made them dangerous.

For the next hour, they all walked together in silence, everyone too full from breakfast and too focused on the switchback trail in front of them to talk, but after an hour, everyone seemed to relax.

Ben broke the silence first. "So why did your mom leave the Rat Fort anyway? This doesn't seem like an easy place to live."

Sarah laughed. "Of course it's not easy, silly. If it was easy, then everyone would live on top of a mountain, and my mom would live down in the village."

"Is that why she left the Rat Fort? To get away from the people?" Kira asked.

Sarah shook her head. "I don't think so. My mom likes people well enough, but she just likes her gryphons more. She left the Rat Fort soon after Grandfather went missing. She said that if he doesn't need to sit on the Rainbow Throne, then she doesn't need to sit in the Rat Fort."

"Did you say gryphons?" Snugg shielded his eyes with his paw and stared up at the mountain peak. "You mean to say there are *real* gryphons up there? I thought they were extinct."

"I thought so too," Fred added, "I haven't seen a gryphon since I was a boy."

"It's no wonder, really. My mom says there are only seven gryphons left in the world." Sarah turned back to face the others. "My mom loves the gryphons, you know—the same way I love my rats. She's the only person in the world who can talk to them using the Indigo Animal Spell. Did you know that? She says it's confusing because half the time you talk like an eagle, and the other half you talk like a lion." Sarah looked up at the mountain. "Not even Grandfather can talk to the gryphons—just my mom."

Now Kira looked up, too. "But why are there only seven left?"

Sarah turned back around, and started up the trail again. "Oh, people hunted gryphons for years. Then, when hunting was made illegal, they poached them instead. Gryphons can be very valuable, you know, because they're magical. For example, any letter written with a gryphon's feather can be sent anywhere in the kingdoms—instantly. And gryphon talons are harder than diamonds and sharper than steel. But the most valuable piece is a gryphon's heart—a gryphon heart can grant a single wish, and that can be priceless."

Kira shook her head. "That's terrible! I can't imagine ever doing something like that."

"Are you sure about that?" Ben whispered behind her. "A single wish would be enough to rescue your mom and dad."

Then Kira understood the temptation. A single wish could do anything. *But would she ever be willing to kill a gryphon to save her parents?*

Kira shook her head. "It doesn't matter. My parents would never want me to save them like that."

The next two hours passed quickly. The switchback trail climbed higher up the mountainside, and the easy conversation once again faded away as the friends walked together in silence. Then, just before midday, the path curved to the left and opened into a large cirque carved into the side of the mountain. The flatland of the hollow was covered in bright green grasses and ringed by dense clusters of pine trees, and at the very center, Kira could see a placid pond of blue water.

Sarah stopped at the edge of the hollow and turned back to the others. "It might be early for lunch, but this is the best place to stop and eat. What do you think?"

Kira nodded. “I wouldn’t mind taking a break.”

The others agreed. They turned off the trail and crossed to the lake. Kira immediately kicked off her sneakers, pulled off her socks, and stepped into the water. It was icy cold, but it felt good covering her feet and splashing against her ankles.

Ben took off his bag and got out the food for lunch. Unfortunately, there was nothing as good as the fish they had for breakfast. They only had bread, lettuce, and a half-dozen tomatoes between them, so Ben did the best he could. He made BLT sandwiches—only without the bacon.

Kira didn’t much care for hers, and after three bites, she handed her leftovers to Fred. Then she rose back to her feet. “I’m going for a walk. I’ll be back in a couple of minutes.”

“Not too far, Princess,” Snugg called after her, and Kira waved her hand to show she understood.

She started walking in the direction of the pine trees. As she walked away from the lake, she couldn’t help but look around at the beauty surrounding her: the towering trees with their dark needles, the long yellow-green grasses blowing in the wind, and the perfect blue water that reflected the mountain peak above it like a mirror.

Kira turned between the trunks of the pine trees, running her fingers over the rough bark, drifting farther and farther away from her friends. She looked back. She was alone now, but she also felt like something was out of place—like somehow she had wandered too far away.

She looked around again, her eyes scanning the ground, and then she saw it: a man's boot-print in the mud in front of her. Someone else was there.

Kira turned back to scream, but before her voice could leave her throat, a heavy hand closed over her nose and mouth.

Then a low voice hissed in her ear, "Don't you say a word."

Chapter 18: Kidnapped

Kira recognized the voice as soon as he spoke. It was Pike. She would know his voice anywhere. Kira tried to scream again, but her voice died inside Pike's hand.

"What did I tell you about that?" he hissed again in her ear. Then Pike spun Kira around and pushed her back against a tree, keeping his hand over her mouth.

He leaned in closer and smiled. "You've cost me a great deal of money, Kira. First you escaped in the forest thanks to that cook. Then you lost me Stony Pointe and the Rat Queen. Those villagers and that girl were paying me lots of money. It's only fair you get it all back for me. There are lots of people in the kingdoms would pay a fortune to own the Rainbow Princess—"

Kira made another noise—not as loud as a scream—it sounded more like muffled talking. But Pike didn't care. He smiled again, showing Kira his pale teeth. "You make one more sound like that, Kira, and you'll wish you hadn't."

Suddenly, a silver blade tapped Pike under the chin, and Kira could hear the man's teeth click together. Pike looked out of the corner of his eye without turning his head, following the length of the blade back to a green-skinned hand. Then he looked up into the face of Fred the zombie.

Fred twisted his blade to push harder against Pike's neck. "With all due respect, the princess doesn't take orders from you."

Then Snugg was standing next to Kira, claws out and at the ready. "You can take your hands off of the princess, or I'll take them off for you."

Pike pulled back his hand, raising both of his arms over his head in surrender. "Boys, I was just talking to Kira about business. You know how it is. A man needs to earn his living."

But now it was Kira's turn to smile. "I was trying to warn you, Pike, to let me go. Maybe next time you'll listen."

Pike laughed. "So we agree there's going to be a next time. That's good to know."

Kira's face hardened. "Tie his hands together, and bring him to the lake."

Snugg darted behind the steam bandit and wrapped his hands with rope. Then all four of them emerged from the cluster of pine trees, Kira and Snugg in front with Pike trailing behind and Fred in the rear, the point of his rapier pressed between Pike's shoulder blades.

Sheriff Quincy was the first to see them. "Look there. It's that steam bandit. He musta been trailing after us."

Then Quincy stepped closer to Pike, jabbing his finger against his chest. "A man like you belongs in jail!"

Kira nodded. "You're right, Sheriff. That's exactly where he belongs, but that may prove trickier than it sounds. We're so close to the mountain top. I don't want to turn back now."

"We could leave him here. Tie him up to a tree or something. That's what he did to you," Ben said.

Kira looked down at the ground. The truth was, she had the same idea, but now, hearing Ben say it out loud, she knew it was impossible. She couldn't leave Pike behind, tied to a tree, helpless to defend himself against wild animals.

"You're right, Ben," she said. "Pike would probably leave us here, but that's all the more reason why we can't do the same to him. Our only other choice is to bring him with us."

Sarah jumped to her feet. "Um, Grand Vizier, I don't think that's a good idea. My mom doesn't like steam bandits, and she sure won't trust this one around her gryphons." Then Sarah covered her mouth with the back of her hand. "They were most of the poachers."

Pike's eyes flashed, and his crooked smile filled his face. "Did she say gryphons? Kira, if that's true—if there are real gryphons up there—I take everything back. Help me get just one gryphon, and I promise, you'll never see me again."

Sarah stepped back, her face red. "How can you say something like that? Why would you ever want to hurt a gryphon?"

"Because they'll make me rich," Pike hissed between his teeth. "I just need one of you to help me. What do you say, cook? Feel like getting rich? Or how about you, Sheriff? Are you interested? Believe me, boys, if we can sell just one gryphon and split the profits between us, we would still be the two richest men in the kingdoms. Trust me—"

"No!" Kira shouted, her voice echoing off the mountain walls. "No one's listening to you anymore, Pike! No one's trusting you ever again! It's like you're already in jail. You just don't know it yet."

Then Pike laughed—a short, mocking sound from the back of his throat. "If that's what you think, Kira, you don't really know me at all. In fact, you don't know me half-as-well, as I know you."

Kira felt her stomach twist over, but only for a second. Then the sick feeling turned to anger. She was tired of Pike playing his games. She was tired of hearing him laugh at her. *And besides, what did any of that mean? How could Pike know anything about her?*

Kira lunged forward, grabbing Pike by his jacket. "How do you know anything about me? How did you know my name?"

Ben and Snugg jumped in, pulling Kira back from the steam bandit, but Pike laughed again—a real laugh this time, rolling from his stomach. "How do you think I know you? I saw your picture—the one with your mommy and daddy climbing that tree. There aren't many girls with pink hair in this world, Kira."

Kira knew exactly the picture he was talking about. It was her mom's favorite: a family portrait hanging in her dining room. But that meant…

"You were in my house?" Kira screamed.

Pike kept laughing. "Of course I was in your house, Kira. Who do you think kidnapped your mother?"

Then everything stopped. There was no noise—no movement. Even Pike's laughing died on the wind. Kira's whole body felt cold and still, like she was a statue trapped inside herself, watching the world around her.

Pike smiled, and his crooked teeth made Kira feel sick again. "Tell you what, Kira. You let me go right now, and maybe I'll tell you the name of the person I sold her to. How's that for a compromise?"

"He's lying, Princess," Snugg growled.

"Snugg's right. We can't trust him, Kira. You know that." Ben put his hand on her shoulder.

Then Kira nodded, but even that movement felt strange—like someone else was nodding her head for her. "We should keep going. Bring the prisoner with us."

*****

The second half of the day's journey felt much longer than the first. From the cirque, the trail grew steeper as it climbed toward the mountain's summit.

It was also more difficult for the companions to find their footing. The scree under their shoes acted almost like marbles. The elevation was a challenge, too—the higher they climbed, the thinner the air—and that made it difficult for Kira to catch her breath. But the worst part of the afternoon was walking with Pike. No one felt like talking or laughing like they did in the morning—not around him. Instead, they trudged up the mountain single-file, in silence.

It left Kira plenty of time to think—too much time, really. At first, she tried to focus on happy thoughts and good memories. She tried to picture the look on her dad's face when she made it to the mountaintop. She tried to imagine how happy she would be to see him again—to hug him again—and what she would say to him, but those happy thoughts didn't last for long.

Even though she tried to focus on her dad, Kira's mind kept jumping ahead to her mom. *Where was she? How would they ever find her? Was she safe?*

Kira remembered what it felt like—waking up, tied to a tree, and listing to Pike's voice from the darkness behind her. She remembered how scared she was. Then she thought about her mom being tied up in some dark dungeon. *Was she scared, too?*

Kira wanted to help. She wanted to save her mom. At the very least, she wanted to let her mom know that she wasn't alone. She wanted to tell her that help was on the way, but Kira knew that was impossible. There was nothing she could do, and that was the worst thought of all.

Finally, just before the sun could dip below the horizon, they reached the mountain top, and there was nowhere left to climb. Just in front of them, Kira could see a small, wooden house. There was a short, tin chimney rising from the back of the roof with a ribbon of smoke curling into the sky, and the front windows were lit with dancing yellow light.

Kira stepped forward. "Should I knock or something?"

Before anyone could answer, the door to the house kicked open, and a tall woman's silhouette filled the doorframe.

She held a lantern in front of her. "Who's out here? Who are you?"

Then the woman made a terrible noise. It sounded like a roar, only louder, and it shrieked and screamed at the end like a thousand nails scratching against a chalkboard. Then there was a loud *whoosh* like a gust of wind, and Kira looked up.

At first it was hard to see—the sky was already turning dark—but Kira could tell that she was looking at something big, almost the size of a car. It seemed to float above the house. The shadow was shaped like a cat—only a cat with wings, and the wings were huge, each one the length of a school bus. The creature hovered over the house for another second. Then it landed on the roof, and Kira could hear the walls of the house groan and creak under the weight. She was surprised the whole building didn't collapse straight away.

Kira could see the beast clearly now for the first time as the light from the lantern fell across it. Its head looked just like an eagle's, crowned with white feathers, receding into brown and finally turning into the golden fur of a lion's body. It had bright yellow eyes and a golden-yellow beak, and its talons curled over the edge of the roof.

The gryphon opened its mouth and roared, and it sounded just like the woman's roar, only louder—infinitely louder.

Then the woman stepped off her porch, peering into the shadows. "Adrianne, go and eat them."

Chapter 19: Gryphons

"Mommy!" Sarah ran forward, waving both of her arms over her head.

"Sarah? Is that you?" The woman raised the lantern over her head, trying to get a better look at the girl running towards her. Then she called back to the gryphon, "Wait, Adrianne. Don't eat anyone—yet."

Adrianne growled from her perch and shook her head. Then the giant gryphon lay down across the roof.

"Mommy!" Sarah shouted again, throwing her arms around the woman's neck.

Then the woman stepped back, pulling herself free from Sarah's embrace. "What are you doing here, Sarah? And who are all these people?"

"Well, we came to see you, and these people are my friends—or they're mostly my friends. There's a mustache-man I don't really know and a steam bandit, but the rest are my friends. Come and see."

Sarah grabbed her mom by the arm and dragged her forward. "Everyone, this is my mom."

Now that she was closer, Kira could get a good look at the woman. She was much taller than Kira's mother, and her face was very narrow with a sharp nose. Her eyes were dark brown, and her hair was mostly black except for curls of blue and purple that twisted down in front of her face. She wore heavy boots and a long green skirt with a brown jacket.

As she stood in front of them, the woman didn't smile—not once. She stared down at the companions, her thin lips pressed together in a straight line.

Kira stepped forward, reaching out to shake hands. "It's nice to meet you, ma'am. I'm Kira. I guess if you're Sarah's mom, that also makes you my aunt. Aunt Indigo, right?"

Indigo looked down her nose at Kira. "Who are you again? My niece, you say?" Indigo turned her head to the left, then back to the right, studying Kira from different angles. "You must be Scarlet's daughter. You look just like her."

Kira could feel her cheeks get warm as she started to blush. No one had ever told her that she looked like her mom before—probably because her mom was beautiful, and Kira looked like… Kira.

She shook her head. "I don't think so—"

"Of course you do. Don't correct me, girl." Indigo reached down and raised Kira's chin to get a better look at her. "Maybe not with your hair, but everything else. You look just like Scarlet when she was your age—even the freckles."

Kira pulled back. "So you *are* my aunt?"

The tall woman shook her head. "I have no idea who you are. Scarlet was my sister, but then she left. I've never seen you before in my life. That hardly makes us family."

Kira's face twisted. "But—"

Indigo turned away. "And who else has Sarah dragged to my home?"

Snugg stepped forward and bowed his head. "Princess Indigo, it's good to see you again."

Indigo looked down at the bear and laughed. "Snugg the Betrayer. Of course you're here. I should have known."

Ben shook his head. "What are you talking about, 'Snugg the Betrayer'? You mean 'Snugg the Destroyer,' right? That's his name after all."

"No, I don't think so." Indigo still stared down at Snugg. "I haven't used *that* name in… Well how long has it been now, Snugg?"

"Twenty years, Princess," Snugg growled. "I've been gone for twenty years."

"And somehow that's still not long enough. I thought you were exiled for the rest of your life, but here you are—still alive. Of course, I shouldn't be surprised that you broke your promise. History and all..."

"Princess Indigo, I—" Snugg tried to answer, but Indigo turned away.

"And who else?" Indigo's eyes rolled over the crowd. "It looks like a zombie, and a scruffy-headed boy, and a mustache-man my daughter barely knows, and a captured steam bandit. Lovely."

Then Indigo drew herself up, somehow standing even straighter and taller than before. "It won't do any good to stand outside in the dark. Come into the house."

Indigo turned back to the house, and everyone followed. As she reached the door, the gryphon lying across the roof raised its head.

Indigo looked up. "Go back to your nest, Adrianne. These are friends, I suppose."

The gryphon gave a short scream. Then she stood up, and with a single flap from her wings, Adrianne lifted off the roof. Everyone stopped to watch the gryphon soar into the air—everyone except for Indigo. She was already back inside her house.

She called over her shoulder, "Come inside and close the door."

Kira followed into the house. The others did the same, and Sheriff Quincy closed the door.

The inside of Indigo's house was small and simple. In fact, it looked to Kira that the entire house only had the one room. On the right side, she could see a table and chairs. At the back of the house was a sink and stove, and on the left side, a set of stairs led to a loft over the kitchen. Kira wiggled her way behind the table and sat down.

"Pardon me, ma'am." Sheriff Quincy pushed back his hat with his finger. "When we were walking in and you spoke to that there gryphon, it understood what you said?"

Indigo looked at Quincy, her eyes narrowing. "Of course she understood. That's why she did exactly what I said. Gryphons are smart—smarter than most humans, obviously—and they're incredibly loyal. Adrianne has a nest behind my house with three beautiful eggs inside. She would do anything for those eggs—*anything*—because that's how gryphon loyalty works. Just like those zombies, am I right?"

Then Indigo turned to look at Snugg. "Some of us could learn a lot from gryphons and zombies, don't you think?"

"You say there are eggs outside?" Pike stood just inside the door, smiling. "You wouldn't mind selling one, would you? I could get us a fair price."

Indigo turned to look at Pike, and for the first time since Kira met the woman, she smiled—but it wasn't warm or friendly. Her lips looked like a pair of worms, their ends curling up in the summer sun.

She stepped closer. "You're the steam bandit that my daughter captured, correct?"

Pike still smiled, his pale teeth reflecting the lamplight. "I wouldn't say 'captured'—more like detained."

"Let me be clear," Indigo's voice fell to a whisper. "If you say anything like that again, I'll feed you to Adrianne as a snack."

Pike still smiled. "Fair warning, Princess Indigo. I don't take kindly to threats. They never really work on me."

Indigo turned away. “How did you even find this man, Sarah?”

Sarah jumped forward, grabbing both of Indigo’s hands. “It was incredible! First there was a battle… No, actually, first, we were on the same side, but then he was lying. It was all a paradox, you see. *Then* there was a battle—”

“Enough.” Indigo pulled back her hands, shaking her head. “It doesn’t matter. It’s all your Aunt Saphron’s fault. *She’s* the one who let these steam bandits run amok over the kingdoms. The problem is that Saphron’s not a leader. Scarlet was a leader. Your Aunt Aileen is a leader.” Indigo shook her head. “Saphron wants to be popular. She wants to be everyone’s favorite, but that makes for a poor leader. She’ll let the kingdoms tear themselves apart as long as people think she’s nice.”

“Maybe she’s trying her best,” Kira blurted out before she could think to stop herself.

Then Indigo turned to look at Kira, her eyes narrowing again. “There are things in this world you don't understand, Niece—a history you know nothing about."

"Maybe not," Kira said, "but I understand you. You're an angry person, and you're mean."

Indigo pulled out one of the chairs and sat down across from Kira, her eyes never leaving the girl. "Well, if you know so much, maybe you can tell me what you're doing here. Have you come to overthrow my sister? You want the Rainbow Throne for yourself?"

"No!" Kira pushed back from the table. "I don't want—I'm here because I want my father."

Then Indigo laughed.

"Why's that funny?" Kira asked.

Indigo's laughter slowly died away. "It's just, you're going to be terribly disappointed, Niece, because your father's not here."

Kira's stomach tightened. It all felt exactly like it did before—first with the Zombies, then with Sarah, and now with the Indigo Princess. Once again, she'd reached the end of her journey only to discover another beginning. Kira wanted to scream. She wanted to slam her fists on the table. She wanted to cry—but she didn't do any of that. She held it all inside, because it didn't matter. Kira would do anything—go anywhere—to save her family. She just needed to know where.

Sarah sat down on the chair next to Kira. "What are you talking about, Momuchka? I sent Uncle Henry here, just like you told me."

Indigo reached out to pat Sarah's hand. "I know you did, Sarah. You did just what I asked. And Henry *was* here—two days ago—but now he's not. I sent him to your Aunt Odele as a wedding gift."

Sarah pulled back her hands and started clapping. "Aunt Odele is getting married? That's wonderful news. And who's the lucky man?"

Indigo sighed, touching her fingers to the bridge of her nose. "We already talked about this last week, Sarah. Odele is marrying Henry's father. She's marrying King Morgus. She's going to become Queen of the Unicorn Kingdom."

Kira stared across the table. "Where's my father now?"

Indigo smiled. "I already told you, Niece. He's back where he belongs. He's home in the Unicorn Kingdom." Then Indigo stood up from the table. "As for the rest of you, I suggest you sleep while you can. I want you gone in the morning."

Chapter 20: Bigger Problems

Kira was still asleep—mostly. Her eyes were closed, but slowly she was becoming aware of the sounds around her. First there was a soft thud, like someone sat down next to her. Then there was a shuffling sound, like someone was dragging their feet over the wooden floorboards. Something was wrong.

Kira's eyes flashed open, and she tried to scream—to warn the others—but a heavy hand closed over her mouth, muffling the noise before it could escape. Then Kira tried to move her arms—to fight back—but she couldn't do that either. She could feel her hands tied tight together behind her back.

A rough hand reached under one of her arms, pulling her up to her feet and dragging her towards the door. Kira tried to turn around—to see who had her—but the hand over her mouth held her in place. She couldn't see anything but the darkness inside the house. Then the door kicked open, and the black shadows of the house turned into the gray light of morning.

Kira was outside now, on top of the mountain. A heavy fog filled the valleys on either side of the mountain peak, and the rest of the Gryphon Mountains looked like tiny islands suspended in a sea of clouds.

Kira's feet dragged over the loose stones. Then the hand pulled her sharply to the right, and Kira spun to the ground, landing hard on her backside.

"Princess, are you all right?" Snugg growled.

Kira looked around. Everyone else from the house was already outside. Snugg, Fred, and Ben all sat to her right, their hands tied behind their backs. Sarah was on her left. She was tied up, too, and Chase the rat was next to her with tiny string wrapped around all four of his legs. Indigo was on the other side of Sarah. She sat hunched over, staring at the ground.

But where was Sheriff Quincy? Kira looked around again, but he wasn't there. Then she looked back at the house. That's when she saw him, standing by the door, looking down at the others. *He* was the one who pulled Kira outside.

"What are you doing, Sheriff?" Kira shouted.

Quincy pushed up the brim of his hat with his finger. "Well, I think we plan on stealin' some gryphon eggs. Maybe do some kidnappin', too. I ain't rightly sure of all the particulars."

Kira shook her head. "You—you joined with Pike? But why? You said you owed us a debt."

Quincy nodded. "Yep, I did. I reckon I still do, but I learned something from Mr. Pike and Mayor Randolph. There's a reason they wanted to get in that sheep's pen. It makes life awful easy. I'm gonna be one of the two richest men in the kingdoms now. You can understand that much, can't ya?"

Kira felt her face flush red-hot with anger. Sheriff Quincy had betrayed them all just to make himself rich, and he was right—Kira *could* understand his reasons, but she would never understand his actions. Snugg, Ben, and Fred—even Sarah and Chloe—they would never do anything like this. Neither would she.

"But you're breaking the law," Sarah said, trying to inch herself closer to Kira. "As soon as we get back to Stony Pointe, I'm going to order you to put yourself in jail."

Quincy smiled. "That's fair enough, Yer Majesty, but I don't plan on going back to Stony Pointe. I might jus' travel 'round with Mr. Pike for a while."

"And where is Pike?" Kira yelled.

"Oh, don't worry, Kira. I'm right where I said I'd be." Pike stepped around the side of the house, and in his hands he held what looked to be an egg—the biggest egg Kira had ever seen, almost the size of a basketball. It was colored bright blue, like a robin's egg, and it was speckled with flecks of white and yellow. Kira could guess well enough where Pike got it.

The steam bandit crouched down to look Kira in the face. “You remember what I said? I told you we’d be here again.”

“You leave that egg alone!” Indigo screamed.

Then Pike stood up, smiling, his pale teeth filling the bottom half of his face. “Oh, Princess, what threats do you have this morning? Not so easy when you’re the prisoner, is it?”

Pike lifted the egg in one hand, turning it left and right. “You said something about this egg last night, didn’t you? How your gryphon would do anything for it? Something about gryphon loyalty.” Then Pike raised his voice, but he wasn’t shouting at Indigo anymore. “I want you to come out here! Now!”

Adrianne stepped into view from around the side of the house. The gryphon walked very slowly with her head bowed low, almost touching the ground. Kira thought she looked defeated.

Pike crouched down again, this time staring at Indigo. “If I told your pet to use you as a snack, you think she’d listen? Should we find out?”

"You can't do that!" Kira screamed. "I won't let you."

"You still don't understand." Pike stood up, laughing. "I get to do whatever I want now—all thanks to this." He held out the egg again in front of Kira's face. "And what I want right now is for the princess to tell me where to find her other gryphons."

Indigo shook her head. "I won't do it."

Pike stepped in front of Indigo again. "Of course you will, Princess. One way or another."

Then Indigo said something else, but Kira was no longer listening. Instead, she edged closer to her friends on the right. "I need to get free. Can anyone cut the ropes?"

"I don't think that's possible, Princess," Fred whispered. "Snugg's already tried with his claws, but the way they tied his hands, he can't reach the ropes."

Kira looked at Ben. "And what about shaping the light? Can you use it to make a knife, or a pair of scissors? Anything?"

Ben shook his head. "I already told you, Kira, I can't—" But then the boy stopped himself. He took a slow breath and forced a smile. "I told you I can't promise anything, but… I'm willing to try. Come over this way so we're sitting back to back."

Kira pushed herself backwards until her shoulders touched Ben's.

"It's difficult," Ben said, "I've never made a knife before, and it's worse because I can't see what I'm doing, either. I'm trying to imagine a dagger. Or some kind of a sword—any kind of sharp blade, I guess."

Kira tried to pull her hands apart, but the ropes held tight. "I don't think it's working. Maybe you're not imagining it right."

"Probably not," Ben whispered, "but I've never really used a dagger. Let me try something else. I'm picturing a kitchen knife now… my kitchen knife. This is the one they gave me when I first learned how to cook. It's got a worn wooden handle and a long blade only sharp on one side. I can almost feel it in my hand."

Kira pulled against her ropes again, and this time they moved. She could wiggle her wrists back and forth. "I think it's working, but it's still not enough."

"I imagine myself chopping onions now, getting ready for the night's dinner… Okay, Kira, try it now," Ben said.

Kira pulled again—harder this time—and suddenly the ropes tore away. "Got it."

"What's that? Did it—did it work? Kira? Did I really do it? You're free?" Ben asked.

"You did perfect, Ben. Now quick, get the others." Then Kira jumped to her feet. "All right, Pike! I think that's enough!"

Pike stepped back from Indigo, turning to face Kira. For a second, his eyebrows knit together in confusion, but slowly, his wide, crooked smile spread over his face.

Then Pike started to laugh. "What do you think you're doing, you stupid, stupid girl? You think I'll keep you safe because you're a princess—because you're worth some money? I don't need you anymore, Kira. I have a gryphon."

Kira balled up both of her fists. "I'm not scared of you anymore, Pike. If I have to fight you, I will."

Pike laughed. "Oh, Kira, I'm afraid you have bigger problems than me to worry about." Then he turned to look at the gryphon. "I want you to rip that girl apart."

"What?" Kira's eye darted from Pike to Adrianne.

The gryphon no longer stared at the ground. Now her head was up, her wings were set back, and her eyes were staring straight at Kira. Her feathers and fur bristled down her back, and then Adrianne gave a short growling shriek.

Kira took a step back and shouted. "Squeak! Squawk! Gryphons! Talk!"

Then she tried to make a sound like a gryphon, but the only noise that came out of Kira sounded more like a squeaky wheel on a grocery cart.

Adrianne turned her head to one side. Then she charged.

Kira turned to run away, but she was already at the edge of the mountaintop, and there was no room to escape—and no time.

Adrianne lowered her head, and she rammed Kira square in the chest, tossing her up into the air, twisting over the edge of the mountain, and falling like a rag doll.

"Princess!" Fred shouted.

Ben and Sarah both screamed, "Kira!"

But it was too late. She was already gone.

Then Snugg growled, "As soon as I'm free, Pike, I'm going to cut you into ribbons."

Pike still laughed. "Your threats don't mean anything, bear. I have a gryphon protecting me now."

"But not for long," a voice shouted.

Then everything seemed to happen at once. Pike wheeled around in the direction of the voice, and everyone else stared behind him.

It was Kira!

She was back. She hovered in mid-air behind the steam bandit, her purple butterfly wings stretched out on either side of her shoulders waving back and forth in the wind. She flew forward suddenly and kicked Pike's arm, hard at his elbow. His hand jerked, and the gryphon egg he was holding launched into the air. For a second, it looked like a mistake—like Kira was *trying* to break the egg—but as it fell towards the ground, Sarah dove forward—her hands cut free from the ropes—and she caught the egg before it could smash against the rocks.

Then Kira's butterfly wings evaporated in a purple mist as her feet touched the ground. "Gryphons are pretty smart, Pike, and this one understood me perfectly. Adrianne did just what I asked her to do, and now her egg is safe."

Pike drew his sword, pointing the blade at Kira's face. "But I don't need a gryphon to end you, Kira. I can take care of that myself. This is the last time you ever rob me of my fortune, girl."

Kira shook her head. "I think you have bigger problems than me to worry about, Pike."

Pike's face twisted. "What are you talking about?"

Then he turned his head—just in time to see Adrianne leap off the ground, her wings spread wide. The gryphon was on top of Pike before he could move—before he could speak—her talons grabbing his shoulders. Then Adrianne beat her wings against the air, climbing higher above the mountain, turning wider and wider over the open sky.

Then she opened her claws, and Pike dropped, twisting through the fog.

Chapter 21: A Letter Home

Adrianne turned through the skies, her golden fur and brown feathers rippling in the wind. She circled the mountaintop twice, roaring into the skies, and then she landed, soft as a feather, in the middle of them all.

First the gryphon looked at Kira, but then her eyes focused on someone else—Sheriff Quincy. Adrianne's fur bristled again, and she leapt forward.

As soon as she jumped, Quincy threw both his hands into the air and dropped to his knees. "I surrender. I-I surrender. Jus' don't toss me off the mountain—please."

Kira stepped forward next to the gryphon, and now they were both standing over the trembling sheriff. Kira reached up, and ran her fingers through the soft feathers on Adrianne's neck, and the gryphon pushed its head against Kira's hand, like a housecat that wants your attention.

Then Kira turned back to Quincy, and her voice was cold. "I think surrender's a good choice, Sheriff. Now stay where you are and think about what you've done. Gryphons are smarter that most of us, and this one won't be happy if you try to escape."

Quincy looked down at the ground. "Yes, ma'am."

Then Sarah and Snugg both ran forward to meet Kira. Snugg jumped into the air, hugging Kira around her neck, and Sarah wrapped her arms around them both.

Fred and Ben got there next. The zombie and the boy threw their arms around everyone they could reach, adding another layer to the group hug. Then even Chase joined them, scurrying up to the top of Sarah's head and dancing for joy.

They all stayed there, laughing and hugging, until finally Fred said, "So that was your plan all along, Princess? To use the Purple Butterfly Spell?"

Kira laughed. "I don't know that I would call it a plan. It was more of an idea—or part of an idea, really. And I wasn't even sure that Adrianne would understand me. Thankfully, she did. She still hit me hard, though."

Kira rubbed her stomach. She was sore from where the gryphon charged her. She was thinking it would be more like a nudge, and then there would be lots of acting on her part—but Kira didn't need to act at all. She was really thrown off the mountain, and it was one of the scariest experiences of her life.

Kira felt someone push against her back. She turned around. It was Adrianne again, rubbing the top of her head against Kira's shoulder. Then the gryphon made a low growl—a noise that almost sounded like a cat's purring.

"She apologizes if she hurt you. She also says thank you for saving her baby.'" Indigo stood off to the side from the others.

Kira turned back to pet the gryphon again. "I know that. I can understand her now."

Then Indigo forced a thin smile. "I guess you can. Most people can't, you know. Not even my father—"

"Sarah told us that," Kira said, smiling, "She told us it's why you love the gryphons so much."

Indigo stepped closer to Adrianne, scratching her fingers up and down across the back of the gryphon's head. "Sarah's right." Then Indigo laughed to herself. "You know, there are only seven gryphons left in the world—seven gryphons, and *those* three eggs. The steam bandits could have had them all—the last of the gryphons gone from the world, but you saved them, Kira. You risked your life, and you saved them all. Your mother would be proud."

Kira's face twisted. It was hard to think about her mom. Just yesterday, she learned that Pike was the man who kidnapped her mother. That meant Pike knew where she was, but now Pike was gone. *How would she ever find her mother now?*

Then a small voice whispered from deep inside Kira's stomach: *You won't. She's gone forever. Just give up.*

Kira shook her head. It was a terrible thought, and she felt guilty for even thinking it, but even more than that, it wasn't true. Kira would never stop looking for her mother. No matter what, she had to keep trying.

Then a warm paw curled around her hand. She looked down. It was Snugg.

"What do we do now, Princess?" he growled.

Kira took a deep breath. "We don't know where my mom is, but we know who has my dad. That's where we need to go next."

"And I'll go too." Sarah jumped into the air and clapped her hands. "It'll be so much fun, like a sleepover—only it'll last for weeks and weeks instead of one night. Then, when we're done, we can go back to the Rat Fort and eat snacks and tell spooky stories."

Fred laughed. "I don't want to spoil things, Your Majesty, but you realize that the Unicorn Kingdom is on the *other* side of the Gryphon Mountains. You'll be traveling farther away from Stony Pointe and the Rat Fort."

"That doesn't matter to me," Sarah said. "I promised Kira I would help her find her dad, so that's exactly what I'm going to do."

"It's not just the distance, Sarah." Indigo put her hand on her daughter's shoulder. "You need to understand that Henry and Scarlet both have enemies in this world. It's going to be dangerous… for all of you."

Sarah smiled. "Of course it's going to be dangerous. That's why I have Chase." Sarah pointed up to her hair, and Chase stuck his head out from the tangled mess and squeaked.

Indigo frowned. "I think it's a bit more dangerous than that. You're going to need more than a rat to protect you—"

"And she does. She has all of us," Ben said, staring back at Indigo. "We're all Sarah's friends now, and our friends take care of each other."

Kira nodded. "That's right. We do."

Indigo shook her head. “I don’t think any of you know what you’re getting yourselves into, but maybe it’s not my place to stop it. Scarlet is *your* mother, after all. Henry is *your* father. My daughter and your friends seem committed to helping *you*.; maybe I should do the same. I can write a letter of introduction, and tell my sister Odele who you are. I’m not sure it’ll do any good, but—”

Before she could finish, Adrianne roared, and then she flapped her wings hard toward the ground. For a second, the gryphon went airborne—but only for a second. As she landed and pulled back her wings, three of the gryphon’s long, russet feathers floated down through the air.

Kira stared at Adrianne. “Are—are you sure about this?”

Adrianne roared again, and then she bowed her head.

Indigo gathered up the feathers from the ground and held them out to Kira. “Adrianne says these are for you—to aid in your journey. They’re very valuable, you know. Gryphon feathers can send a letter—"

"—anywhere in the world," Kira finished, taking the feathers. "Sarah already told us. But how do they work? Do I need an address?"

Indigo smiled. "They're magic feathers, Kira. You don't need an address or a stamp. You just write your letter in the air, throw the feather into the wind, and the magic will take care of the rest."

Then a slow smile inched across Kira's face, and she couldn't stop it from spreading. "I know who I'm writing first."

Kira took one of the feathers and held it in her hand like a pencil. Then she started scribbling through the air like she was a kid playing with a sparkler on the Fourth of July. Gold letters and words hovered in front of her face only to disappear a second later. Finally, when she finished writing, Kira threw the feather into the air like a dart.

Suddenly, a sound like thunder ripped through the sky, and everyone on the mountaintop jumped in their skin and ducked their heads. Then the feather was gone, lost in an explosion of orange sparks.

Kira looked back at her friends. "Time to get my dad."

*****

Scarlet sat in the dark room on a pile of damp straw, her back pressed against the stone wall and her face cradled in her hands. She had no way of knowing how long she had been there—how many days it had been since she was stolen from her home—but it didn't matter. Whatever the real length of her stay, Scarlet knew her time in the room felt even longer.

She pushed her dark red curls back from her face and looked around the dungeon again. Nothing had changed. Aside from the damp straw, the only other furniture in the room was a wooden bucket left in the corner, and the only other decoration was the locked door on the far side of the room. The door itself was simple—dark, heavy wood with a tiny window and bars at the top. Scarlet hated it.

She braced her hand against the wall and slowly rose to her feet. Her whole body felt weak, but she couldn't let herself think about that now. She couldn't think about the locked door, or the damp straw, or how long she had been kept prisoner. She had to find something positive to focus on—something like standing. At least she could still stand up. She could walk around the room if she wanted, and that was something, too.

Scarlet forced herself to smile. "They could have chained me to the wall."

Just then, a sound like thunder ripped through the tiny room, shaking the walls, the floor, and the ceiling. It was enough to throw Scarlet sideways, back into the pile of straw. Then, in an explosion of sparks, a single brown feather appeared floating in the middle of the room.

It hovered toward the wall, and then it started writing all on its own. It scratched across the wall, and everywhere it touched, delicate gold words burned against the stone.

Dear Mom,

I know you're scared, but try to be brave. I'm going to rescue Dad, and then we'll find you and save you together. I miss you very much, and I love you forever.

All my love,

Kira

"What's that, Scarlet? A letter from home?" a silky voice purred through the window in the door.

Scarlet shook her head, staring at the locked door and the dark window. "It's not from home. It's a letter from my daughter. She's here, and she's coming to save me."

The voice on the other side of the door laughed. "I've heard all about our dear, sweet Kira, but she's only a child, Scarlet. I'm not afraid of her."

Scarlet smiled. "That's because you don't know Kira."

Acknowledgements

The more I write, the more I realize how impossible a task this would be without the love, support, and encouragement from my friends and family. They have all shared in my struggles as I've chased my dream of writing, and so it's only right that I acknowledge them here and invite them to share in any future success I might enjoy.

First, as always, I need to thank my incredible wife Vanessa. She has made this novel possible through her endless patience and encouragement, and I am so grateful to share my life with her. Likewise, I want to thank my children, Aidan and Fiona, who are always ready with boundless ideas to send my imagination soaring in new directions. I may be the one putting words to paper, but the story of Kira belongs to them.

I also want to thank my trusted team of "beta-readers" who offered their insights and loving criticisms to help me forge the best story possible. My team this year includes my brother Michael and his wife Nan, my sister Courtney Ader, and my friends Lindsey DeVol, Curtis Homan, Jeffrey "Danger" Krachun, and the eponymous Sarah Weng.

Once again, I am indebted to the efforts of Liam Carnahan and his team at Invisible Ink Editing for correcting my mistakes and sharpening my story. I am a better writer today thanks to working with Liam. I also want to thank Kike Alapont for creating another amazing cover for my novel. He seems to understand my characters just as well as I do, and it was a joy to collaborate with him again.

For more information about my writing and the future adventures of Kira Turner in the Rainbow Princess Chronicles, please visit my website at:

www.jasonrjames.com